D1134971

Six Feet Undertow

Elizabeth Penney

CountrySampler®
CountrySamplerFiction.com

Six Feet Undertow
Copyright © 2016 Annie's.

Library of Congress-in-Publication Data
Six Feet Undertow / by Elizabeth Penney
p. cm.
I. Title
2016955017

CountrySamplerFiction.com
(800) 282-6643
Antique Shop Mysteries™
Series Creator: Shari Lohner
Series Editors: Michelle Ochoa, Janice Tate and Ken Tate
Cover Illustrator: Bonnie Leick

10 11 12 13 14 | Printed in China | 9 8 7 6 5 4 3 2 1

1

Maggie Watson wasn't sure what woke her first—the cat's nose touching hers or the sunshine streaming through the drapes she had neglected to close completely. Together they were enough to jolt her thoroughly awake.

"Cut it out, Snickers," she said with a laugh as the tabby's whiskers tickled her cheek. Sitting up in bed, she gently nudged him aside. She glanced at the bedside clock, which read six o'clock. "Don't tell me you're hungry." With a sigh, she flung back the covers and slid to the edge of the bed.

Then Maggie remembered. Her daughter, Emily, had left for college yesterday. She stopped moving—one leg out of the covers, the other in—as scenes from Emily's visit flashed through her mind. She cherished the memories, holding them close against the fact that, yes, she missed her daughter—even if she was incredibly proud of her and glad Emily was so self-sufficient and independent. It was just the two of them now; Maggie's husband, Richard, a college professor, had died a few years ago.

"Thank goodness she's not one of those boomerang kids," she said to Snickers with a shudder. "Some parents I know have permanent residents in their basements."

Snickers nudged her arm with his head and mewed.

She stroked him gently. "You miss her too, don't you?" Whenever Emily showed up, Snickers trailed her day and night, even sleeping in her room instead of on Maggie's bed. After a final pat, Maggie thrust her feet into slippers and stood. "Well, enough of that. It looks like a beautiful day." She strode to the wide window and opened the drapes fully, revealing a breathtaking ocean view.

That vista was a bonus Maggie had enjoyed every day since moving into the nineteenth-century Colonial Revival mansion left to her by her late aunt, Evelyn Bradbury. Sedgwick Manor was not only huge and luxurious, but it was also stuffed with the antiques and memorabilia that had been her aunt's passion, an enthusiasm Maggie shared. Evelyn had turned her passion into a successful business, Carriage House Antiques, and now Maggie and the shop's longtime manager, June McGillis, operated it.

Maggie took a deep breath, savoring the view of the sunlight sparkling on blue water under an almost cloudless sky. September in Maine was beautiful, with warm days and plenty of sunshine. Far out to sea, a tanker slowly chugged its way north. How fascinating and beautiful the view must have been when four-mast schooners and clipper ships were a daily sight. The sea captain in her family tree, Thomas Sedgwick, had traveled the world in such a ship. He had built Sedgwick Manor for his wife, Abigail.

A breeze sprang up, rustling the leaves of the maples edging the lawn. Maggie noticed something alarming. One of the trees was tinged with red. Winter was announcing its imminent arrival.

"All the more reason to enjoy autumn while it's here. Wouldn't you agree, Snickers?" The cat wound around her legs, clearly eager for his meal. "All right, all right. But after I feed you, I'm getting dressed and going out for breakfast. To The Busy Bean."

After showering, Maggie threw on jeans and a long-sleeved T-shirt, sneakers, and a light jacket for the walk down to the café and coffee shop. Owned by her friend Daisy Carter and located by the docks, The Busy Bean was one of her favorite spots in her adopted town of Somerset Harbor.

The café wasn't far away, the walk exactly long enough to get her blood pumping as she strode down Shoreline Drive. As she drew closer to the café, she noticed a crowd gathered outside, which was unusual since the tourist season was nearly over. In addition, there were cars parked up and down the street, and she thought she spotted a television truck with its rooftop antenna. *What on earth is going on?* She picked up the pace, eager to find out.

"I wondered when you'd get here." Ina Linton, Maggie's seventy-something friend, stood at the edge of the crowd. Tiny with hair like dandelion fluff, Ina was known for her forthright tongue and unusual outfits. Today she wore a navy blue sailor suit with a neckerchief, square collar, and wide-leg pants.

Maggie put her curiosity about Ina's outfit aside for a more pressing question. "What's going on?"

Ina pointed to a handsome middle-aged man pushing through the crowd to a podium placed to one side of the parking lot. He had wavy blond hair and twinkling blue eyes. "Don't you recognize him? That's Benton Lee, the star of that treasure-hunting reality show, *Deep Sea Secrets.*"

Maggie studied the man. He looked vaguely familiar, but she had never watched the show. "What's he doing here in Somerset Harbor? We don't have any treasure, do we?"

Ina wagged a finger. "That's where you're wrong. Benton is here to raise the *Abigail.*" At Maggie's startled expression, she added, "That's right. The ship owned by Thomas Sedgwick. She went down offshore in 1864, remember?"

"I remember hearing something about his ship sinking, but I didn't know exactly where it went down." One of the most interesting stories Maggie had learned upon inheriting the mansion and reading Evelyn's antiques-and-history notebook was that after Thomas's death, Abigail Sedgwick had left the main house and secluded herself in a small cabin. No one seemed to know exactly why.

Then Maggie put two and two together and felt a jolt of excitement. "Are you telling me there was treasure on board?"

Ina grabbed her arm. "Hush, he's going to start speaking."

Benton waved, giving the crowd a wide and infectious grin. "How y'all doing today?" He spoke with a pronounced Southern accent. The crowd roared in greeting. "As many of you know, I'm Benton Lee, host of *Deep Sea Secrets*." He paused for applause. "I'm here in town with my fabulous crew"—he gestured to two men standing nearby—"and we're planning to put your charming little town on the map."

Ina snorted. "It's already on the map. Has been for centuries."

Benton pointed toward the harbor. "Yes, we're going on a real treasure hunt right here, out in those frigid Maine waters. We're going to use the *Deep Six*, our state-of-the-art ship, to scour the rocky bottom where the *Abigail* and her cargo lie, far out of anyone's reach—until now."

"Folks have tried," Ina muttered to Maggie. "But they didn't have any luck. Didn't find a thing."

Maggie's pulse raced at the realization that her ancestor's ship had allegedly been carrying valuable cargo. Why hadn't she known about this? He was a distant relative, after all. She'd have to go through her aunt Evelyn's notebook again. Maybe she had missed something.

"Tell us about the treasure!" someone shouted from the crowd.

"My colleague will do that in a moment." Benton gripped the edge of the podium and gazed around at the upturned faces. "But first my cohost, Rory James, is going to talk about our unique ability to retrieve precious items from the ocean floor."

The man who stepped forward was bald, burly, and deeply tanned. "G'day, mates. I'm Rory James." Hoots and applause rippled through the crowd. Maggie remembered that Rory used to be on an Australian wildlife show called *Animals Down Under*.

"I'll bet they have to powder that head under the lights," Ina said, referring to Rory's shiny dome.

"Benton mentioned the *Deep Six*," the Australian was saying. "She's a marvelous tub, outfitted with all the latest technology that allows us to see the ocean floor as clearly as we can see the surface of this parking lot." He gestured at the asphalt. "All that stuff, laid out for us to pick over, thanks to Spot, our robot. We call him Spot because he fetches, you see." He paused for laughter.

"Previously, investigating a wreck like the *Abigail* wasn't possible." He slapped the top of the podium. "But now it is, and we're here to do that for you." He jabbed a forefinger at the host. "Take it away, Benton."

Benton stepped forward again. "Some of you might be wondering why we've kept the mission hush-hush until now."

Maggie was wondering that herself. Surely Benton should have contacted her at Sedgwick Manor to see what she knew about Thomas Sedgwick and the *Abigail*.

"Although the story of the *Abigail*'s sinking in September of 1864 is well-known, it is considered legend by some. After all, Captain Thomas Sedgwick was a naval captain with an inherited fortune, so why would he have a treasure aboard? And as I said earlier, the wreck is in a highly inaccessible spot, perched precariously near the edge of a huge underwater cliff. A few feet more . . ." Benton shook his head sadly.

"We came up here this summer under the radar—so to speak—to map the ocean floor with sonar. To our delight, we discovered what we're convinced is the shipwreck. Now we're here to explore the remains." He nodded at another man standing nearby. "And after Professor Addison Stringfellow speaks, y'all will see why we've been so secretive."

With a wave, the tall and gangly professor stepped up to the microphone. With his pointed nose, wire-rimmed glasses, and thinning sandy hair, he didn't have a tenth of the media presence of Benton or Rory. But when he opened his mouth, it seemed everyone hung on his words.

"We believe the *Abigail* is holding millions in gold," he announced bluntly. "Gold stolen during a bank robbery in Boston on September 12, 1864."

Maggie almost swooned. Captain Thomas Sedgwick had been involved with a bank robbery? Was that why Abigail had cut herself off from society, out of guilt and shame?

Addison continued, "Although the exact role of Thomas Sedgwick hasn't been determined, the identities of the bank robbers are well documented. They were a group of Confederate soldiers."

Ina frowned. "I didn't know Confederates came this far north into Yankee territory."

"Me either," Maggie said. Everything she had read about the Civil War focused on Union troops venturing into the South.

"These soldiers were bound for Canada," Addison said, "to seek assistance for their cause. On the way, they ran into a terrible storm. The ship foundered and was lost. There were no survivors." He bowed his head, silent for a moment, an effective technique that created a sense of sorrow and reverence for the tragedy.

A strident voice broke the silence. "The *Abigail* was jinxed! And it's still jinxed. Plunder her at your own peril!"

2

The onlookers broke into a hum of conversation as all the cameras swung toward the person responsible for the outburst. Maggie recognized him as one of the old salts who hung around the docks, Clem Jenkins.

Benton chuckled. "Thanks for pointing that out, sir. Nearly every wreck we've salvaged was rumored to be either haunted or jinxed. But our team, with the help of Spot, has managed to succeed anyway. We'll do the same with the *Abigail*."

Clem harrumphed and crossed his arms. "You better pray you're right."

"I know I'm right." Benton pointed at Clem, smiling like he was bestowing a huge favor. "And you're invited to join us for the first trip out on the *Deep Six* to the site."

"You ain't getting me out there, no way." The old man shook his head with a scowl.

Judging by the media's jostling for pictures and the frantic note-taking Maggie witnessed, they were eating it up. The rumors of a jinx would only add to the story's allure, which already had "legs," in reporter lingo. Lost gold, a treasure quest, and a reality television crew added up to a big story in Maine. Maybe it would even go national.

"Suit yourself." The television star gave the crowd a jaunty wave. "That's all for today, folks. Ladies and gentlemen of the media, please contact my company for any interview requests. Benton Lee Productions. We're on the Web." He stepped down from the podium and made his way toward The Busy Bean's door, stopping on the way to say hello and shake hands with fans.

"Let's go in," Ina said. "I think you should meet Mr. Benton Lee, since he's going to be picking the bones of your ancestor's ship."

"I hope we can get in there." Maggie looked around and, to her relief, she noticed that the crowd was thinning, most of the audience wandering down the street or getting into vehicles and driving away.

As they walked toward the café, Maggie glanced at Ina's outfit with new understanding. "Now I know why you're wearing that. It's in honor of the treasure hunt."

Ina grinned as she adjusted her neckerchief. "That's right. This suit belonged to my uncle, who served in World War II. He was a small fellow, but brave."

"I'm sure." Maggie realized something else. "But that means you knew about this before I did."

Ina put her hands on her hips. "Well, if you'd have answered your phone this weekend, I would have told you. I read about it online, that they were coming here."

"I'm sorry. I was busy with Emily."

"That's okay. I also heard about it from Robert. Not everyone has that advantage." Ina's nephew worked for the Somerset Harbor Police Department. She gave a wave. "There he goes now."

Officer Robert Linton was pulling away in his cruiser, the presence of law enforcement a requirement for any event on public property like the docks, which belonged to the town.

Maggie and Ina pushed their way into the coffee shop, the bell on the door jingling. The place was standing room only, Maggie saw with dismay. The owner, Daisy Carter, was busy behind the cash register, ringing up customers. Southern transplant Daisy, with her bouffant hairdo and friendly charm, didn't appear to be breaking a sweat handling the rush—until she noticed Benton approaching the counter.

Daisy's mouth dropped open and her eyes lit up. "Benton Beauregard Lee. Get your big ol' handsome self over here." She darted around the edge of the counter, running toward Benton with outstretched arms. Apparently Daisy had already met Benton, and judging by the bear hug and affectionate kissing of both cheeks, she knew him quite well.

Ina darted a look at Maggie. "Well, isn't this one for the books?"

Harry Carter, Daisy's husband, appeared in the kitchen doorway. By the perplexed expression on his face, Maggie could tell he was equally taken aback. He stopped short, eyes fixed on the man embracing his wife.

Using both elbows, Ina forged a path through the cluster of bodies wedged between the door and the counter. The sight of an elderly woman wearing a sailor's uniform caused enough astonishment and interest for people to step back without protest.

Hands on hips, Ina swiveled her head between Daisy and Benton, who were still regarding each other fondly. "What in tarnation is going on here?"

Daisy gave a girlish giggle, unusual for the middle-aged woman. "Ina, this here is my college beau." Her Southern accent seemed to have thickened. She slid her hand through Benton's arm. "I haven't seen him for a whole lot of years." She giggled again. "I'd say how many, but then you'd know my age."

"We already know that," Ina snapped. "It's no secret around here. Fifty-eight and counting."

Benton's eyes twinkled as he patted Daisy's hand. "This is the one who got away. I'm not sure why I ever let that happen."

"Me neither, sugar, but you did." Daisy let out a big sigh and shook her head. Spotting Harry, she gestured for him to come over. "Benton, I want you to meet my husband. He's the one who *didn't* get away." As Harry joined them, Daisy dropped

Benton's arm and took Harry's, beaming proudly. "I won this restaurant in a contest, believe it or not. When I moved up here to Maine to claim my prize, I met Harry Carter—the biggest prize of all. It was the best day of my life."

Benton's face fell slightly, but he recovered and shook Harry's hand. "I'm happy to meet you, Harry. Glad to be here in your lovely little town."

Harry appeared to be mollified by his wife's words, and he replied courteously, "Welcome to Somerset Harbor. We're excited to see what you manage to salvage from the *Abigail*."

"Hopefully you'll get all that gold, every last piece of it," Ina said. "I'm Ina Linton by the way, a Somerset Harbor native. Anything you want to know, just ask me." Grabbing Maggie's arm, she pulled her forward. "And this is Maggie Watson. Thomas Sedgwick's cousin was her ancestor, and she lives in the manor Thomas built for his wife."

Benton eyed her speculatively, rubbing his chin with one hand. "Why don't we take a seat? I'd like to talk to you about your family."

"I'm warning you, I don't know much," Maggie said. "I lived most of my life in Vermont, and I've only recently started researching my family tree."

"Let's talk anyway. What would you and your friend like?" Benton placed his order with Daisy, then ushered them to a recently vacated table overlooking the water. Daisy brought their order over right away—the cook's famous egg sandwiches and a round of coffee and water.

"I'll get you the catering menu shortly," Daisy said to Benton. "We'll be able to do your breakfasts and pack box lunches for your team when you're out on the boat."

Benton added three teaspoons of sugar to his coffee. "Thanks, Daisy. We're all staying at the Oceanview Hotel, so they'll fix our meals on days we're not sailing." He winked. "I'll see what I can do about getting The Busy Bean a line in the credits for this episode."

Daisy put a hand to her chest. "That would be wonderful. Are you sure you can do that?"

"Of course. It's my show, darling." Benton watched as Daisy happily sashayed across the room, stopping to chat with other patrons. "Daisy Mae sure is a great gal."

"She really is." Maggie took a big bite of egg sandwich. It was way past her usual breakfast time, and she was famished. Benton and Ina appeared equally hungry, and they all ate in silence for a few minutes.

Benton wiped his mouth with a napkin. "Tell me what you know about your family, Mrs. Watson." He focused his attention on Maggie with a flattering intensity.

Maggie gave him a brief overview of her family's arrival in Maine. "Thomas Sedgwick built Sedgwick Manor, where I live."

"It's spectacular," Ina said. "One of the town's most beautiful structures."

"Really?" Benton rubbed his chin again. "Maybe we can include some shots of it." He snapped his fingers and pointed at Maggie. "I'd like to do an interview with you for the show. You can talk about your family history and Thomas Sedgwick. I'm sure viewers would be interested to see where he lived."

Butterflies began churning in Maggie's belly at the idea of being filmed. She didn't even like having her picture taken. "But I don't know much about Thomas." She hoped that would dissuade him. "I'm sure you can find an expert somewhere."

Benton grimaced. "No, I've got enough experts around. We want the personal touch. Tell me what you do know and we'll go from there."

Maggie filled him in about Abigail's self-imposed isolation after Thomas's death. "She stayed in a cabin on property that belonged to the Sedgwicks at the time. My late aunt never told me why. Now I think it might have had something to do with the shipwreck."

"It wouldn't go well for Confederate sympathizers in Maine," Ina said. "So you're probably right. Maybe people thought Abigail was involved and gave her trouble."

"I can look through my aunt's notebook and papers to see if she knew anything else," Maggie said. "I'd be happy to share." And if she didn't like what she learned, she wouldn't tell Benton.

"Excuse me." They looked up to see an attractive blonde in her midthirties looming over the table. She wore a jacket adorned with the logo of Portland's Channel 5.

"Stella Marquez." Benton rose to his feet. "Why are you here?"

Maggie thought that was a strange greeting.

Stella flipped her hair back over her shoulder, smiling smugly. "Hi, Benton. I left the network a few months ago. I work for a Portland channel now."

"I didn't know that. How nice to see you." He introduced Maggie and Ina to Stella, who was his former colleague.

"Glad to meet you both." Stella turned her blinding white smile on Maggie. "I'd love to interview you for *Seacoast Today*, my weekly magazine show."

Ina made a startled sound. "I watch that show. That's a huge opportunity." She elbowed Maggie. "Say yes."

"What do you want to interview me about?" Maggie had watched the show too, and it featured a wide variety of stories, from true crime to historic buildings to Maine cuisine.

"Your ancestors, of course. Thomas and Abigail Sedgwick, their tragic love story cut short by the shipwreck carrying Confederate gold."

Ina whistled. "Put that way, it is quite a story."

Maggie had to agree. It had all the ingredients—romance, tragedy, wartime, and scandal.

Benton broke into their conversation. "I'm sorry, Stella, but Maggie is going to appear on my show. I can't have you scooping my story."

Stella bared her gleaming teeth. "Ever hear of a little something called freedom of the press? Well, I'm the press, and I'm free to pursue whatever story I want."

Maggie ducked her head while the reality show host and the reporter engaged in a glaring contest. How had she become the subject of a competition between media outlets? For two cents she'd finish her coffee and run home, then bar the door against them both.

"Tell you what, Stella," Benton said. "Let's meet for dinner tonight at the Oceanview and chat about this. I'm sure we can come to some arrangement that will meet both our needs." Maggie glanced up to see Benton beaming the full force of his charm at Stella.

Stella smoothed her hair into place, her eyes never leaving Benton's face. "All right, Benton. We can do that." She fished around in her pocket and gave Maggie a card. "I'll be calling you, Maggie."

After she walked away, Benton said to Maggie, "I'll have my office send over a contract for you to review later today or tomorrow."

A contract? Eek. "Um, Mr. Lee, I'll have to think about it." Maggie attempted a chuckle. "I'm not exactly a television personality."

"Don't worry about it. I can tell already you'll look good on camera. Plus I really want you involved in the show. I think you'll bring a unique perspective." He got up to leave. "Trust me, Maggie. This would be a great move for you."

After breakfast, Maggie put the interviews out of her mind

and walked toward the manor on winged feet. She couldn't wait to dig into Evelyn's notebook and see what she could find out about the *Abigail*.

She had almost reached the manor driveway when an SUV slowed to a halt beside her, June at the wheel. The passenger window rolled down. "Good morning, TV star," June called across the empty seat, a huge grin on her face.

Maggie put her hands on her hips. "How did you hear about that already? You weren't at The Busy Bean, were you?" She hadn't seen June there, but the place had been packed.

"No, I wasn't. But Ina told Ruth, who called me on my cell." Ruth Harper was the president of the historical society and another good friend.

Maggie shook her head. The Somerset Harbor news network was faster than the speed of light. "Despite what Ina says, I haven't decided if I'm going to be on the reality show. Or *Seacoast Today*."

"It would be fun. And a television appearance will help promote the shop." June winked. "But no pressure."

"I hadn't thought about that, but you're right." Carriage House Antiques did well, but appearing on television would be free advertising. "I'll think about it."

"Like I said, no pressure. Do what feels right." June glanced at her dashboard clock. "Oops. Time to go open the shop."

"I'll be over in a while. See you soon."

June sped off, slowing to turn onto the separate driveway leading to the antiques shop while Maggie headed up to the mansion. One of her main concerns about appearing on television, she realized, was how Thomas Sedgwick would be portrayed. Maggie didn't believe for a minute that he'd participated in robbing a bank. She'd seen far too many shows where someone was put on the hot seat to boost ratings, and she didn't intend to be that person.

Inside the house, Snickers ran to greet her, and after an extended petting session, the duo went to the kitchen, where Maggie put on a small pot of coffee. While the coffee brewed, she looked in the fridge for dinner ideas. She found a package of stew beef, so she quickly chopped onions, potatoes, and carrots and threw them into a slow cooker. The browned beef, spices, and broth followed. Later she would add fresh mushrooms and frozen peas.

Feeling virtuous about what she'd accomplished, Maggie poured a mug of coffee and went to the office. She loved sitting behind the beautiful flame mahogany partners desk to do paperwork. Like the rest of the mansion's rooms, this one was furnished with eclectic but original antiques, and she savored having them around her.

She stored Evelyn's journal in the desk, in the same drawer where she had found it. Evelyn had kept a record of the purchases she made along with notes about their history. Maggie had found one section focusing on Sedgwick heirlooms and collections, so she turned there first. She leafed through the pages once, then again. *Ah, there it is, under the* Figurehead *listing. Did Aunt Evelyn mean the figurehead from the* Abigail? Maggie read the entry, which like most of Evelyn's notes was all too brief, often resulting in more questions raised than answered.

It began with a quote, something Maggie remembered reading in Shakespeare. She read:

> *"Done to death by slanderous tongue*
> *Was the Hero that here lies."*

Interesting. The note then said that Abigail had been a fiercely loyal woman, driven into seclusion after Thomas died.

Maggie already knew that much. What she lacked was information as to why. Had people believed Thomas was a criminal, part of the Confederate gang that had robbed the bank in Boston? That would have been quite a scandal during the Civil War in a Union-supporting state.

Then dismay iced her core. *Had* Thomas been involved in the crime? No, it couldn't be. Evelyn's quote referred to slander. If only Maggie could prove he was innocent before the scandal was dredged up along with the ship's cargo.

There was a little more to the entry.

> *Does the figurehead hold the key? It is the one artifact to survive the Abigail's shipwreck. Must research.*

Apparently Evelyn had never gotten around to digging into the mystery. Now it was up to Maggie to clear Thomas's name and prove that Abigail's faith in her husband had been justified.

3

"I think the historical society should help you clear Thomas's name." June placed a captain's hat on a desk next to a sextant and spyglass. Behind the desk hung an antique painting of a four-mast schooner in heavy seas and a mariner's clock. "I don't believe he robbed a bank or was a Confederate sympathizer. Good grief."

"I'm glad you agree with me." Maggie helped June wrestle a heavy standing globe into place. Following Evelyn's decorating legacy, June and Maggie arranged shop items in new vignettes every month. The displays always spurred sales and made the shop look nice. "I didn't know we had so many nautical things in stock."

June studied the arrangement, her head cocked. "I thought it would be fun to acknowledge the reality show while they're in town." She pursed her lips. "Unless you'd rather not. I didn't think of that."

"It's fine. We can't do anything about the salvage operation. Lost treasure on the ocean floor is fair game."

June crossed her arms and tapped one foot, thinking. "So you're not going to put in a claim as the owner of the *Abigail*?"

"If I did, it would be for *Abigail* artifacts that belonged to Thomas. Certainly not for the stolen gold. Although a show like that costs millions, you know, I suppose they could afford to part with a little sunken treasure," Maggie joked. She had spent a few minutes looking up Benton and his former treasure hunts, most of them quite successful. However, such an operation required huge sums of money, most of which came from backers who expected a share of the findings.

Maggie glanced around the shop. "You've never come across anything from the ship, have you, either here or at the house?" If anyone knew the inventory and Evelyn's collection, it would be June.

"Everything went down in the storm, as far as I know. Is there anything in particular you have in mind?" June made a final tweak to the display, then stood back to study it.

"Evelyn's journal said a figurehead survived." Idly, Maggie spun the standing globe, which depicted the world 150 years ago. How many of the seven seas had Thomas traveled?

"A figurehead? I haven't seen one." June walked toward the tall bookcase holding classics in the back of the room. One of the decorative touches June favored was a short stack of leather-bound books. "It would be wonderful to find it, though. They're usually beautiful, quite artistic."

Maggie followed to help choose books. "How do you think the historical society can help? Is there information in the collection about the *Abigail*?" During former research projects, Maggie had looked through their collection and visited the local newspaper archives and the library.

June patted her arm. "You know us. We'll dig something up. Besides the usual sources, there are attics all over town holding pieces of our history."

The door opened and James Bennett entered. The tall, handsome Somerset Harbor alderman often repaired furniture for Carriage House Antiques as part of his restoration business.

"Good afternoon, Maggie, June." He shrugged off his jacket and hung it on a peg beside the door.

"Hi, James." Maggie gave him a little wave, feeling a smile break out across her face. She couldn't help it; she always felt a jolt of excitement when James entered a room. *He is just a good friend,* she reminded herself once again. Richard had only been gone for a few years, and she wasn't ready by any stretch to move on.

"Are you here about the inlaid chest?" June asked. "I put it in the back room."

"Yes, I'd like to check it over and see what I need for supplies." He brushed his dark hair back from his forehead, sending Maggie a mischievous grin. "I'd also like to congratulate our resident television personality."

Maggie felt a flush heat her cheeks. "Cut it out. June said the same thing. I haven't decided whether or not I'm going to be on TV."

James looked astonished. "Why not? It would be a great way to promote the antiques shop. You'd get free national exposure."

June nodded in agreement. "That's what I said. We can't afford to buy that kind of advertising."

Maggie dropped her gaze to the edition of Kipling's *Captains Courageous* she held. "I'm not sure I want to support the theory that Thomas Sedgwick was a bank-robbing criminal. And you know they'll focus on the salacious details—television always does."

James laughed. "Maggie, that was over a hundred years ago. No one cares anymore."

Maggie thrust out her chin stubbornly. "I do. And June said the historical society will help me clear Thomas's name. I hope you'll get on board with that. I'm sure we could use your help." If James couldn't understand the importance of learning the truth about her family history, especially as someone who was so passionate about history himself, then she would really be disappointed.

To her relief, he nodded. "Of course I will. I'll do anything I can to help, you know that. Maybe Mother has something in her attic that will shed light on the subject." Deborah Bennett was a kind woman who was always willing to lend a helping hand, like her son.

Maggie's heart sang. "Thanks, James." Then she thought of something. There was a source they hadn't considered. "I wonder what that professor Addison Stringfellow knows. Apparently, he's the consultant for this project, and he seems to know a lot about the bank robbery."

"Good point, Maggie." June took the Kipling from Maggie's hands and added it to the ancient volumes of *Moby Dick* and *Robinson Crusoe* she held. "Maybe you should talk to him."

"Keep your cards close to your vest when you do," James said. "Try to get information from him without giving any. Then you can stay in control of the story."

Maggie regarded James with appreciation. "Great advice. Thanks."

"A reporter I know uses that technique." James glanced at his watch. "I have another appointment this afternoon, so I guess I'd better check out that cabinet." He headed for the back room.

June set the pile of books on the desk next to the captain's hat. "I have an idea, Maggie. Why don't you host a gathering for the television crew at the manor? I'm sure they would love to see it, and it would be a perfect opportunity to discuss the project."

Maggie considered the suggestion and quickly warmed to the idea. "I'll have a dinner party and invite the historical society members too. Will you help me? I haven't hosted a big event in a long time."

"I'd love to." June gestured for Maggie to follow as she moved toward the front counter. "Let's make a list of guests and a menu. We'll give Benton and his friends a wonderful taste of Maine hospitality."

. . . .

"I've got the bisque from The Lobster Quadrille," Daisy said, bustling through the mansion's back door, holding a big brown paper sack in her arms. Daisy, June, and Ina were helping Maggie with the dinner party, and at that moment the kitchen and dining room were a flurry of controlled mayhem.

"Thanks. Put it on the counter right here." Maggie pulled out a large soup pot and set it next to the soup. She unrolled the top of the bag and reached inside for the containers. Everything else on the menu was homemade, but nothing could beat the Quadrille's lobster bisque.

"What can I do?" Daisy slipped out of her coat.

"Pull out a peeler and help me with these potatoes." Ina stood near the sink, a heap of potatoes at her elbow.

"I can do that." Daisy opened the utensil drawer and found the tool.

Maggie set the pot of soup over low heat on the stove to keep it warm. Her next move was to preheat the oven for the baked haddock dish.

June hurried into the kitchen. "I've got the tablecloth and napkins on. Where's the silverware?"

"In the top hutch drawer," Maggie said. "I thought we'd use the real silver tonight. And the gold-rimmed china in the hutch too." Both had belonged to Aunt Evelyn, and until now, Maggie hadn't had an occasion to use them.

"Gotcha." June dashed back out.

"There's trouble in paradise." Ina plunked a peeled potato into the pot. "I read that Rory James was passed over for the lead host role and he doesn't like it one bit."

Daisy made a scoffing sound. "Reading gossip magazines again, Ina? You can't believe anything they say."

"Where there's smoke there's fire, I always say." Ina picked up another potato.

"But isn't it Benton's show?" Maggie asked. "*Deep Sea Secrets with Benton Lee.*"

"True. But you see, Rory has more TV experience. Benton was working as a treasure hunter before he got tapped to do the show."

"He studied to be a marine biologist in college," Daisy added. The peel she was carving made a perfect spiral. "Guess treasure hunting pays better."

"Sometimes." Ina nodded sagely as though she were an expert on the subject. "Benton is the one who brought in the financial backers." She threw Daisy a sly grin. "You better watch out, Daisy. I also read that Benton and his wife are on the outs."

Daisy stopped peeling the potato, her mouth dropping open. "Why, Ina Linton! What's that got to do with me?"

Ina pursed her lips. "Like I said, where's there's smoke . . . Benton seemed awfully enamored of you the other day."

Daisy blew air out through her lips. "I assure you, he's not. And I'm not interested in him in the slightest. I'm happily married, and my relationship with Benton is water under the bridge—ancient history."

"What's ancient history?" June walked back into the kitchen.

Ina and Daisy looked at each other. "Nothing," they said in unison.

"All we need to do now is light the candles and we're all set." June looked around. "What do you want me to do out here?"

Maggie dredged the fish in a butter-rich mixture of crumbs, garlic powder, parsley and other herbs, and lemon peel. "After I get this ready, I'll do the salad next. Want to help with that?"

"Sure," June said. "I'll pop into the powder room and wash my hands."

"So who all is coming tonight?" Ina asked. "I feel like I'm working KP in the army." She picked up the huge pot of potatoes and placed it on the stove.

"Us, of course, plus Harry, Kurt, Fran, Ruth, James and Deborah Bennett, the Youngs, Benton plus his date—"

"Benton is bringing a date?" Ina's nose fairly twitched with curiosity. "Who?" To Daisy, she whispered loudly behind her hand, "Sounds like you're off the hook."

Daisy rolled her eyes as she scooped the potato peels into the garbage can.

"Benton didn't say. Anyway, Rory and Addison are coming too, so that makes sixteen." Maggie beamed at her friends. "Thanks again for your help. I haven't fed this many people in a long time."

A few minutes later, the doorbell rang, announcing the first guests, Ruth and Fran. Both were members of the historical society. Maggie got them settled in the formal living room with glasses of the sherbet punch she had made for the occasion. As if they'd led a caravan, Ruth and Fran were followed quickly by Maggie's other friends in Somerset Harbor.

"Everyone looks nice tonight," Maggie said to the room at large. The men were in sport coats and dress pants, and the women wore nice dresses or pantsuits. The air held faint traces of perfume and cologne along with the scent of a crackling applewood fire.

Standing next to her at the mantel and looking handsome in charcoal gray, James flashed her a grin. "So do you, Maggie."

Maggie felt her face flush. "Thank you." She hadn't worn her autumn suit—a dark green faux suede skirt paired with a brocade jacket—since the last time she'd attended a faculty party with her late husband.

"It's nice to have an excuse to dress up," said Fran Vosburg, owner of The Quilt Cupboard, a quilt shop downtown. At thirty-six, she was also the youngest member of the historical society.

"That's right," Ruth Harper said. She glanced around at the clusters of lit candles and vases of autumn flowers set here and there in the two-story room. "Everything looks wonderful."

"June did most of the decorating," Maggie said. "So all the credit belongs to her."

Standing a short distance away beside her husband, Kurt, June smiled and lifted her glass in acknowledgement.

"Where's the TV gang?" Harry asked, looking slightly uncomfortable in his Sunday best. As a lobsterman, he usually wore dungarees or canvas work pants topped with a sweater and oilskins.

Maggie glanced at the mantel clock. Almost twenty minutes past the time she had given Benton. "I guess they're fashionably late." The food was almost ready, timed for a short drinks period before being served. Much longer and the fish would be ruined—crisp dry blocks rather than tender and flaky filets.

Apparently gripped by anticipation, Maggie's guests were much less lively than usual. They broke into two clusters, men and women, and chatted quietly, discussing mundane topics. Maggie felt herself beginning to steam. *How inconsiderate of Benton and his companions to be late.* She was ready to suggest they start to eat without them when the doorbell rang.

Setting her punch on the coffee table, she left the room and walked past the stairs. The front door was directly in view of the formal living room, and behind her, all the chatter ceased. She sensed everyone was watching her and the door, eager to see the guests of honor.

Benton, Addison, Rory, and a tall blonde woman stood on the porch. For some reason, Maggie had expected Benton to bring Stella Vasquez, the reporter. This woman was older but equally attractive, with refined features and a trim figure.

"Good evening. I'm so glad you could join us." Maggie stood back and ushered them inside.

"I'm terribly sorry we're late, Maggie," Benton said. "But—"

"It's all my fault, Miss Maggie," the blonde woman said.

She had a strong Southern accent. "I was late getting to the hotel. Forgive me?" She flashed an ingratiating smile and batted her obviously false eyelashes.

Someone shrieked, and Maggie heard the clatter of heels on the hall floor behind her. She turned to see Daisy bearing down on the group, red-painted mouth gaping open and her hands flapping.

"I can't believe it! Meredith Crenshaw!" Daisy looked the other woman up and down, taking in every detail. "We were sorority sisters, Maggie." She turned back to her friend. "You're looking well, Merry."

Meredith gave an icy little laugh. "Please don't call me that, Daisy. It's Meredith *Lee* now. No one's called me Merry in ages. How ridiculous." She handed her coat to Maggie, looking Daisy over as well. "How's life in Maine, Daisy?" Her tone implied it couldn't possibly be good. "I was surprised when Benton told me he ran into you."

James had also entered the foyer. To Maggie's relief, he was now herding the men toward the living room for drinks, leaving the women to their reunion.

"Oh, I adore living in Maine. Come on, I want to introduce you to my sweetie pie. He's the catch of the coast." Daisy took Meredith's arm and for a moment, it appeared the other woman might resist. Then she gave up and let the brightly chattering Daisy propel her toward the living room.

Maggie followed, trying to shake off the tension brewing between Daisy and her old friend. *Ina's gossip magazine article about Benton and his wife must be wrong, or else why would she be in Somerset Harbor?*

In the living room, James had already introduced the male guests, and Daisy was doing the same with Meredith. Ina's brows skyrocketed when she learned she was meeting Benton's supposedly estranged wife, but fortunately she kept her surprise to herself. Daisy's discreet step on Ina's foot might have helped with that.

James also took over the duty of offering drinks to the new arrivals, so Maggie and June escaped to the kitchen to put the final touches on dinner. Luckily the food was still fine, not dry or overcooked.

At last they all sat down, Maggie at one end and James at the other, and dinner began once Pastor David Young had said grace. As guest of honor, Benton was seated to the right of Maggie, with Rory to her left. "This is wonderful." Benton nodded toward his hostess as he scooped up a spoonful of bisque. "Nothing like fresh Maine seafood."

"I'm glad you like it," Maggie said. "I can't take credit for that, however. A local restaurant made the bisque. Everything else is homemade, though."

June, seated next to Benton, said, "You must sample all kinds of exotic food during your travels around the world."

"That's true, we do," Rory said. "Of course, coming from Down Under, it takes a lot to surprise my palate." He turned to Daisy. "One of my favorites is alligator. Have you tried it, love?"

Daisy threw back her head and laughed, a gesture that drew attention from the others, especially Meredith and Harry. "Why, yes I have. When I was in Florida. Some fiend made me eat it on a dare." She winked at Benton. "Remember, Benton?"

Benton chortled with her. "I sure do, sugar. Alligator on a stick, it was called."

Rory appeared disconcerted at the turn the conversation had taken, but he rallied. "Aren't you an adventurous lass?"

"She certainly is." Benton's smile was fond. Perhaps feeling the daggers in Harry's gaze as well as Meredith's, he changed the subject. "Rory, will the *Deep Six* be arriving tomorrow as scheduled?"

Rory picked up his glass and swirled the contents. "Sorry, I haven't heard anything from the captain yet."

Benton shook his head. "We've had more problems lately . . . but no need to dwell on that." He turned to Maggie. "Is there any chance we could get a tour of the house? I'm interested to see where Thomas Sedgwick lived. It will give me a feel for the man."

"I'd love to give you a tour after dinner." Maggie pushed back her chair with a nod to June and Ina. "Please excuse me. We're going to bring in the next course." While Ina and June cleared the soup bowls, Maggie prepared plates of the main meal in the kitchen. The salads were going to be served with the fish, via two big bowls to be passed around.

Ina giggled with glee as she trotted into the kitchen, carrying a stack of bowls. "I haven't felt so many undercurrents since I was out at the shoals. Woo-ee!" She piled the bowls in the sink.

"What do you mean, Ina?" Maggie asked, handing her two plates to carry.

Ina buzzed back to the kitchen door. "Harry is fit to be tied, Meredith and Rory are in cahoots, and Benton is clearly worried about something. Better batten down the hatches, ladies. I predict stormy seas ahead."

4

"How did she get all that during the soup course?" Maggie asked June, who had entered the kitchen while Ina was talking and set her own stack of bowls in the sink.

"I have no idea, but she is pretty perceptive." June picked up two plates and headed back to the dining room after Ina.

I need to be more observant, Maggie decided. Her focus had been on making sure her guests were enjoying the food, not on keeping track of the dramatic implications hidden in every exchange.

After the main dish was served, Maggie joined the others in the dining room. As they tucked into the fish, she kept a casual eye on everyone. She intercepted one or two glances between Meredith and Rory, and Harry was unusually quiet, even for him. The conversation appeared to be stalled, and she was racking her brain for a topic when Ina spoke up.

"So tell me, Professor, where did you get this nonsense about Confederates robbing a bank in Yankee territory?" Ina cocked her head like a bright little bird.

Addison gave a dry laugh as he pushed his spectacles up with his thumb. "It's all well documented, ma'am."

"Do tell," Ina said. "I'm all ears."

With that invitation, the professor was off and running, and as a result the group learned more than they cared to about the movements of Confederate soldiers throughout New England and the battle fought in Vermont, the northernmost Civil War conflict. Maggie listened intently, hoping to learn something that would clear Thomas from his suspected involvement. Addison's discourse, interrupted with questions from the historical society members, took them through the rest of dinner.

"We do have dessert and coffee," Maggie said, "but perhaps we can have that in the living room after the tour. Who wants to go?"

"I'll clear up and get the coffee and dessert ready," June said.

In the end, Maggie led Benton, Meredith, Rory, and Addison through the house while Maggie's friends helped clean up and then gathered in the living room again.

"This is a beautiful old place," Benton said as they finished their circuit of the downstairs and climbed to the second story. "I hope you'll let us film your interview here. That would add so much depth to the story of the *Abigail*."

"Especially the library," Addison said. "I'd like to include that portrait of Thomas Sedgwick in the shot."

"I'll think about it," Maggie said. "Thanks again for the offer. And you can use the portrait whether or not I'm in the show." She still hadn't decided if she wanted to appear on television. She needed to find out more about how Thomas would be portrayed before she agreed to an interview.

"The rooms in this place are huge," Meredith said, going to the hallway balcony to gaze down at the living room below. A few people glanced up at the tour group and waved. "This reminds me of my family home in South Carolina." Then she curled her lip in derision. "Our whole house in California, on the other hand, would fit in your living room."

"That's because a shoe box costs a million in Los Angeles," Benton said. "And that's where we have to be based for the show."

"Well if—" Meredith seemed to think better of saying more and dropped back slightly to walk beside Rory as Maggie showed them the bedrooms.

Addison especially seemed fascinated by the house, poking his long nose into corners and opening closet doors, all the while muttering under his breath. "You don't have anything from Thomas Sedgwick's sailing days, do you?" he asked when they were headed back to the main floor.

"Not a thing." It was on the tip of Maggie's tongue to tell him about the figurehead mentioned in her aunt's journal, but she managed to keep that to herself. "I haven't even seen a picture of the *Abigail*."

Addison patted his chest pocket, giving that dry chuckle again. "I have one."

Maggie felt a thrill of excitement. "Really? Where did you get it?"

"I was fortunate to discover a painting of the *Abigail* in a marine museum here in Maine. The curator allowed me to take a photograph of it."

The group joined the others in the living room, where June, Daisy, and Ina had set out plates of mini-tarts and a coffee tray.

"Help yourself," Maggie said.

Shortly after dessert, Fran and Deborah politely excused themselves and left, along with the Youngs.

Maggie offered more coffee to Benton and his friends. After they were settled, she said to Addison, "I'd love to see the photograph." To the rest of the room she said, "Addison found a painting of the *Abigail*."

"That's wonderful," June said. Everyone murmured in agreement.

Seated in a wingback chair near the fire, Addison made a show of pulling out the photograph and passing it to Maggie first. "I had a print made rather than keep it only as a digital file."

Maggie studied the painting. It showed the boat in stormy seas, common in paintings of the era. She squinted at the bow. There was a figurehead, tiny in the picture, but maybe she could get it enlarged. "I'd love to have a copy of this. Digital is fine. Would you e-mail it to me?" It would actually be easier to examine a digital copy. She passed the photograph to June, who curled up the corners of her lips ever so slightly. June understood her interest.

Someone's phone chimed. Rory reached into his jacket pocket. "Ah, good. It's the captain," he said to Benton. Rory stepped across the room to talk. "Yes?" A few moments later he returned to the group. "I'm sorry to tell you this, mate. The ship might not be here for a couple more days."

Benton made a muffled sound of exasperation. "Why not? I thought you said Captain Percival knew his stuff, Addison."

"He does," Addison said and turned to Rory. "What's going on?"

Rory shrugged as he slid his phone back into his pocket. "Something about the motor. And he's still looking for crew. One guy he hired got into a car accident last night."

"Could it be the jinx kicking in?" Ina said, her eyes bright with excitement.

"Ina. Don't say that." Daisy's tone was reproachful.

"I don't believe in such things." Benton waved away the idea of a jinx like he was swatting at a fly. He turned to Harry. "You have a boat, right? Would you be interested in taking a few of us out to the shipwreck site tomorrow?" He paused. "For hire, of course."

"We won't charge you." Daisy patted her husband's knee. "It would be our pleasure to help with the project."

Harry didn't look like he agreed with that assessment. "I'll have to wait and see." Daisy gave him an elbow. "I'm saying that because the weather is supposed to deteriorate tomorrow afternoon. You don't want to be out in the *Daisy Mae* in rough seas."

Meredith made a small snort, putting her hand to her mouth to hide a fit of amusement. "You have a boat named after you, Daisy? Why, bless your heart."

From Daisy, Maggie knew the Southern phrase "bless your heart" served to convey a whole host of meanings. In this case, it was not a compliment.

By her friend's wide, fake smile, Maggie knew Daisy had picked up on the subtext and was rising to the occasion. "I was honored when Harry named his newest lobster boat after me," she said sweetly. "This way we're always together, even when he's out on the water. Boats are often named after loved ones or inspired by close personal relationships here in Maine, where we treasure each other." When Meredith snorted again, Daisy, feigning innocence, turned to Benton. "What inspired the name *Deep Six*?"

Meredith flushed at the jibe, shifting in her seat with a little huff. Ina gave a hoot of amusement.

"Doesn't that phrase refer to a certain depth at sea?" Ruth asked. The president of the historical society had been rather quiet all evening, her eyes bright behind her glasses as she took everything in.

"That's right, Ms. Harper," Benton said. "The name is my attempt to add a little levity to our work. In addition, it can refer to something discarded, often at sea." He turned to Maggie. "As the Sedgwick heir, I'd like you to come out with us when we retrieve artifacts from the wreck." He snapped his fingers and pointed at her. "In fact, why don't you come out with us tomorrow?"

Harry cleared his throat and crossed his arms. Daisy patted him on the shoulder. "Benton, I think we'd better wait and check the weather tomorrow. Harry's concerned about it."

"All right," Benton agreed. "We can discuss it in the morning. I'll give you a call, Harry."

Harry still looked disgruntled, and Daisy attempted to mollify him. "I'm dying to see the shipwreck spot. It will be fun."

"If you say so, dear. It will have to wait until after we pull traps in the morning." Harry's Maine accent, always stronger under pressure, broadened the vowels of "dear" and "morning."

The decaf coffee carafe gurgled as James depressed the top button. Maggie jumped up. "I'll refill that."

As she hurried out of the room, Meredith stopped her. "Can I trouble you for the ladies' room?"

"Down the hallway, to the left." Maggie pointed to the location of the powder room. In the kitchen, she brewed another pot of coffee, glad she had bought a regular maker so she had an alternative to single-serving pods. Those were hard to make for a group. Expensive too.

Finally the maker gave its last burp, and she poured the steaming coffee into the carafe and screwed on the lid. She picked it up and hurried toward the kitchen door, only to be distracted by conversation outside in the hallway. She quickly recognized Rory's Australian accent. "Don't worry, love. I'll take care of it. Be patient."

Not wanting to eavesdrop, she continued into the hall. Rory and Meredith huddled together more closely than was appropriate. When they saw her, they broke apart, color rising in Meredith's cheeks. Maggie thought of Ina's words. Were Rory and Meredith up to something?

She smiled at the duo, pretending she hadn't heard a thing. "There's more coffee if you want it."

· · · · · · · · · · · · · · · · ·

"Kurt and I had so much fun last night," June said the next morning at the shop. "I think we'll host a dinner party soon ourselves."

"I couldn't have done it without your help. Or Daisy and Ina's." Maggie leafed through a catalog from an upcoming auction in Camden. "There's some good stuff here. Shall we go?"

"Definitely. That house has been in the same family since the 1800s." June clicked away at the computer, and the nearby printer began to hum. Every morning, she printed an activity report for the previous day.

"Like Sedgwick Manor." Maggie turned to the cover. "It looks like a sea captain's house too. See the widow's walk up top?" Sedgwick Manor didn't have that feature. Had Abigail watched for Thomas's ship from the attic window, perhaps?

"Poor Abigail." June shook her head. "I keep thinking about her finding out that her husband's ship was carrying stolen gold when it sank. What a shock on top of the grief of losing him."

The shop door opened with a jingle of bells and television reporter Stella Marquez blew in, her energy preceding her like a force field. "Good morning, ladies." Her smile was blindingly white. "How are you today?"

"We're fine," Maggie said. "How are you?"

"I'm great." Stella's bright gaze darted around the shop, taking everything in. "What a charming little place!" She stopped to peer at a pair of Victorian lamps with gold trim, then a 1700s washstand complete with a matching basin and pitcher. "Yes," she said as she arrived at the counter, "I could definitely do a show here."

That was fine, except Maggie hadn't decided if she was going to allow Stella to film one. "I'm glad you like the shop."

"I do. And I'd love to feature anything you have that relates to Maine's history."

"We do have a lot of pieces from the area," Maggie said. "But I'll defer to June—she's the expert."

Stella turned to June. "Will you show me around?"

Maggie trailed along while June showed Stella a Samuel Ranlet tall case clock, a delicate black Windsor chair made locally, a hand-painted hope chest, and a marine chart depicting the New England coast from the Bay of Fundy to Block Island.

"I can practically feel the wind in my hair," Stella said as she studied the last item. "A close-up of this chart would be perfect with the nautical display you've set up for a segment about the Sedgwicks." She gave Maggie puppy dog eyes. "Won't you please consider it?"

"You're right, Stella. It would be a great show." June threw Maggie a pleading look of her own. "And great advertising."

Maggie felt cornered, but somehow—rather than cave in as was her usual response to pressure from people she liked—she managed to temporize. "I'll think about it, Stella."

Stella's face fell. "Not for long, I hope. The story is hot right now."

"Please give me another day or so and I'll get back to you, I promise."

The reporter nodded. "When you can." She glanced at her phone. "Oops. I'd better go. I have a meeting at the historical society with Ruth Harper."

"No one knows more about Somerset Harbor than Ruth," Maggie said. "Thanks for coming by."

"I'll be back." Stella paused at the door. "If not to film, then to buy. You really have wonderful things." With a wave, she was gone.

"I'm not going to pressure you, Maggie," June said, "but I really think you should consider Stella's request. Offers of TV appearances don't come along every day."

The fax machine behind the counter made its usual grumbling sounds, and paper spewed into the tray. Maggie reached it first, curious to see who had sent the communication. She quickly scanned the contents, picking out the key points.

"Don't happen every day, you say?" She waved the pages at June. "This is a contract from Benton's company. They want to pay me to be on his show."

Maggie's cell phone rang and she set the papers down to grab it, noticing a number she didn't recognize on the screen. "Hello?"

"Maggie? Benton Lee here. We're heading out to the shipwreck site in an hour. Can you come with us?"

Harry must have agreed to let them use his boat. "I'd love to."

"Meet us down on the docks." He paused. "By the way, did a contract come across your desk yet?"

"I got it right before you called." Maggie felt the squeeze of pressure again. "I'll have to look it over."

"Absolutely. Have an attorney review it if you want. That's what most people do."

An attorney? Maggie hadn't thought of that. She could ask Constance Taylor, the attorney who handled Aunt Evelyn's estate, for a referral.

"I'll do that, Benton. See you in a few." She hung up, then scrolled through her contacts for Constance's phone number. After a brief conversation with to-the-point Constance, she called the lawyer Constance recommended, who told her to fax the contract right over.

A group was waiting on the docks when Maggie arrived. Her heart skipped a beat when she saw the tall figure of James Bennett among them.

"What are you doing here?" Maggie asked him.

"I was in the Bean and Daisy dragged me along." His blue-gray eyes twinkled. "Not that she had to twist my arm. I'm excited to see the shipwreck site."

Harry was already in the red-and-white lobster boat, moving

coils of rope and extra lobster traps out of the way. "We're all set, folks. Let's make it quick." He glanced up at the sky, which to Maggie's eyes looked perfectly blue and placid. "Weather's going to change."

"We'll do that, mate." Rory was the first aboard, and he reached out a hand to help Daisy in, then Maggie. Addison, Benton, and James clambered aboard.

Daisy pulled a scarf out of her coat pocket and tied it over her hair. "It gets cold out on the water," she said to Maggie.

Maggie put on a scarf as well, then braced her legs as Harry started the motor and backed away from the dock. She hadn't gone boating very often since moving to Somerset Harbor, and she enjoyed the view of her new home from this angle.

Buildings lined the waterfront and extended up into the low hills behind the town. She picked out Old Faith Chapel's white steeple, the imposing town hall, Sedgwick Manor, and the lighthouse.

"Pretty, isn't it?" James came to stand beside her at the railing. As the town receded, they turned to look at the islands dotting the bay. As Daisy had promised, a brisk wind pushed at their heads and shoulders, carrying the scent of salt and fish.

After they had motored into the bay for a while, Harry throttled down the engine and began to move much more slowly through the water. Now that they weren't cutting through the waves, the powerful push of the tide began to roll the boat slightly. Overhead, a scrim of clouds was creeping in, slowly overtaking the blue.

"See those waves breaking?" James pointed. "There are rocks under the water right there. If the tide was low right now, you could see them."

"Deadmen's Shoals," Harry called. "Many a wreck has gone down here."

Benton moved to stand beside Maggie and James. "That's where the *Abigail* sank. Foundered against those rocks and broke apart."

Maggie imagined the panic and fear that Thomas Sedgwick and the other sailors must have experienced when they realized they had run aground so far from shore and safety. "Did the storm push them off course?"

"It must have," Benton said. "The shoals are well marked on the charts. And you'd think an experienced sailor like Thomas Sedgwick would have known these waters like the back of his hand."

That's right, he would have. Had he steered the ship onto the rocks on purpose? Maggie shuddered as she gazed at the waves breaking against the submerged hazard. The shore appeared as a distant line of green and blue hills from here. Had Thomas prayed to reach land, to reach Abigail?

She shivered again. The wind had picked up, buffeting the boat and sending a piece of metal gear clanging against the side. The clouds were thickening visibly, rolling in like the breakers below.

"We're in for it now!" Harry gripped the wheel, attempting to keep the boat steady in the increasing chop and rising wind. "Daisy, get the PFDs."

Daisy crouched down and opened a hatch. She pulled out red life vests and yellow slickers and tossed them to everyone on board, including Harry, who managed to shrug into his garments one-handed while still steering.

Maggie slipped into a life jacket, zipped it up, and tightened the buckles. "Having to put these on is not a good sign," she muttered to James. She pulled on a huge slicker over the jacket and snapped it shut, thankful for its protection against the waves and spray.

"It's a good thing we have them." James grabbed the rail as the boat began to pitch and yaw. The breakers were about three or four feet high now, making the boat rise and fall along with the peaks and troughs of gray-green water. Harry's expertise was the only thing keeping the craft upright.

"I guess Harry was right about the weather," Rory said to Benton.

"It appears so." Benton dodged a wave splashing overboard. "I'd forgotten what it's like out on rough water in a small boat."

With the increased rocking of the boat, it was difficult to remain standing in one place. Maggie found herself staggering sideways into James and after the second time, she gave up and sat on the deck cross-legged.

The lanky Addison was also having trouble remaining steady on his feet. After one huge wave hit the boat broadside, he tripped and fell right against Benton. In turn, Benton hit the rail, almost toppling overboard. Fortunately, Rory managed to grab Benton's jacket and haul him back to safety. After that incident, the trio also sat.

Daisy was standing in front with Harry, and Maggie heard snatched words as she called the Coast Guard on the radio. Cold dread hit Maggie like a blow. They must be in *real* trouble, in danger of being swept out to sea or swamped by the enormous waves.

James leaned over, his blue eyes staring fiercely into hers. "Brace yourself, Maggie. The wind and waves are forcing us east."

They were headed straight for Deadmen's Shoals.

"**B**ring her about, mate!" Rory called. "We're headed for the rocks."

Harry shook his head, the irritation on his heavy features conveying quite plainly that he didn't need to be told his business. "I'm doing the best I can. The motor is at its limit."

Despite her desire to stay hunkered down in the boat and hide, Maggie lifted herself up high enough to keep an eye on the shoals, which approached and receded as the boat fought the waves and wind. Rain began to slash down, whipping her cheeks with icy needles. Black clouds boiled above, extending to the horizon.

"It's a storm, Lord," she whispered, thinking of the disciples in the boat on the Sea of Galilee.

"The tide is coming in," James said, "so we should be headed west, toward shore. But the combination of the current and the wind keeps pushing us back."

This must be what had happened to the Abigail, Maggie realized. The shoals had their own microclimate, a trap for the unfortunate and the unwary.

"Does that lobsterman know what he's doing?" Addison asked James. The professor's face was a pale shade of green, and he was grasping his midsection.

"There's no one better," James said. He repeated these reassurances to Benton and Rory, both of whom were also clearly worried. Rory kept muttering to himself, and Benton's eyes were bleak.

The battle between the boat and the weather went on until Maggie didn't understand how Harry could continue to struggle at the wheel. Then, like a miracle, the wind suddenly dropped, and a break appeared in the clouds directly overhead, a tiny blue flag of hope. Harry seized the opportunity and gunned the engine, sending them farther north and out of the current's clutches.

From there it was a matter of turning the bow toward shore, and the boat practically surfed in on the powerful breakers racing toward land. Once they were out of danger, the tension gripping the group dropped away, and the visitors began to joke and laugh. Harry, however, maintained his grim stance as he focused on the harbor ahead. Daisy stood supportively beside her husband, calling the Coast Guard to give them the all clear.

"That was a close one," James whispered to Maggie. "Harry deserves a medal for pulling that off."

"He certainly does. He saved our lives." Now that she could relax, Maggie allowed herself to imagine the headline that might have been printed: *Sedgwick Heir Lost at Sea While Seeking Ancestor's Shipwreck.*

As Harry brought the boat alongside the wharf, Daisy said, "Leave your slickers and life jackets here. I'll hang them up to dry."

Maggie shed the outer garments quickly, noticing that she was soaked through her clothes and her sneakers squished with water. "I can't wait to get home and warm up," she told James. A breeze hit her wet skin and she shivered.

"Me neither." James clambered off the boat and held out his hand to help her. As she stepped onto the blessedly solid concrete wharf, Maggie decided she had never been so grateful to stand on dry ground. She felt like kneeling down and kissing it.

As the others climbed off the boat, Harry called, "Benton, can I speak to you for a moment?"

Benton stayed behind with Harry and Daisy. Harry was silent until the rest of them were out of earshot and walking across the public parking lot, but when Maggie glanced back, she saw Harry in a heated discussion with the television personality.

"Harry's mad that Benton insisted we go out in the boat today?" James guessed.

"It looks that way," Maggie said. "Who can blame him?"

Rory whistled. "I thought we were goners for sure, on our way down to Davy Jones's locker."

"I'm glad you can joke about it," Addison barked. "As for me, I'm headed back to the hotel for a hot bath and a nap. My nerves are shot."

"Sorry, mate—" Rory began, stopping abruptly when a man in fisherman's foul-weather gear stepped into their path from behind a convertible van.

Maggie recognized Clem Jenkins, the man who'd warned them about the curse of the *Abigail* when Benton had first come to town. Clem pointed a long skinny finger toward them, resembling the grim reaper dressed in oilskins.

"I told you TV people that the shipwreck is cursed," Clem said. "You'd better listen if you don't want to end up on the bottom." His drawling Maine accent made his cryptic words even more eerie. "That's right, the bottom, swimming with the fishes."

Addison put his hands on his hips and glared, eyes narrowed behind his glasses. "Are you threatening us? Because I am not to be trifled with."

Clem scoffed. "As if I had anything to do with the weather." He jabbed his finger at the sky, which was now clearing. "What do you suppose all that was about?" He nodded. "A warning."

Addison and Rory shook their heads in disbelief as they veered off to an Audi sedan parked a short distance away. Maggie and

James continued on together, reaching James's Mercedes first. She paused while he dug out his keys.

"What do you make of that?" James tilted his head toward Clem's small figure heading toward the *Daisy Mae*, no doubt to spread his cheer to the Carters.

"He probably just likes the attention. You can't have a decent treasure hunt without threats of doom." Her comment made them both laugh.

James sobered. "Seriously, though, I'm grateful we made it back to shore. I was praying the Coast Guard would get there before we went under."

"Me too." Maggie shivered. "That wasn't exactly the way I'm hoping to go."

"I'm holding out for dying in my sleep at the ripe old age of ninety myself." James unlocked his door. "Do you need a ride home?"

"No, I'm parked over there. Thanks, though." Maggie felt a twinge of disappointment at having to turn down his offer, even if it was only for the short trip to Sedgwick Manor.

"Any chance you're free for dinner? The Oceanview has a great fish-and-chips special tonight."

A rush of pleasure coursed through Maggie, warming her despite her bone-deep chill. "That sounds wonderful."

"Great. How's six sound?"

"Perfect. I'll see you then." Maggie's waterlogged sneakers sloshed as she walked toward the car, her spirits soaring. Her original plan had been to take a hot shower and huddle in front of the fire with Snickers and a good book, but she'd gladly abandon that excitement to spend an evening with James.

. . . .

When Maggie checked her cell phone for messages—after

her shower and a change of clothes—she found two surprises. The first was a message from the attorney saying the contract looked fine as is. The second was a text from Emily that read, *MOM. CALL ME!!!*

Immediately her heart jolted with fear at this urgent summons from her daughter. Had something terrible happened? During class sessions she and Emily generally spoke only on weekends. With shaking fingers she dialed Emily's number.

To her relief, Emily picked up right away. "Mom!"

"Emily, are you all right?" Maggie blurted. "I saw your text—"

"I'm fine." Emily's voice took on a tone of mock reproof. "When were you going to tell me they're filming a treasure hunt involving the Sedgwicks' boat?"

Maggie realized she hadn't filled Emily in—about anything. "I take it you saw the news broadcast about the reality show."

"I sure did. Including Ina's white head bobbing in the back of the crowd." Emily giggled. "Was she really wearing a sailor suit?"

"You know Ina. She loves to get into the spirit of things. Anyway, there's more. They want me to be on the show."

Emily let out a deafening squeal. "Sorry. But that's so exciting! Are you going to do it?"

Maggie thought of the contract with trepidation. All she had to do was sign her name and she would be on national television. "I think I am. Not that I want to be on camera or anything, but they think Thomas Sedgwick was in cahoots with those bank robbers. I don't believe it, and I think someone should stick up for him. And everyone keeps reminding me how it'll be great advertising for Carriage House Antiques."

"I don't believe Thomas was a criminal either. In your portrait of him, he looks like such a stern and stuffy old guy, the kind who never did a thing wrong in his whole life. Abigail didn't seem like much of a troublemaker either. Thanks for letting me hang her portrait in my room while I was home, by the way. She had such a sweet face. It was nice to think she was watching over me while I slept."

"Oh, that's right! I forgot to put it back in the library."

"Did you?" Emily giggled. "It's hanging near the fireplace in my room. Thomas is probably getting lonely without her."

Maggie hadn't included Emily's room in the tour or else she might have been reminded of the portrait. She headed out of her room for the stairs. "I'm going to go move it back."

"Are you climbing the stairs?" Emily asked a moment later.

Puffing with the effort of racing upstairs, Maggie achieved the landing with relief. "How could you tell?"

Emily's room was down the hall, a pretty room with wisteria wallpaper. Maggie opened the door and scanned the walls. Yes, right beside the fireplace hung the photograph of Abigail.

"There you are." Maggie moved closer to study the portrait with a new curiosity for Abigail Sedgwick. Abigail's features lacked the stern demeanor of her husband; her pretty face was oval with neat features. Her dark hair was styled in a large, low bun and she wore a high-necked black dress.

"Isn't it neat?" Emily asked, making her jump. Maggie had forgotten she was on the phone.

Maggie had a thought. "Evelyn didn't mention this portrait in her notebook. Maybe there are other things belonging to Abigail around the house." *Like a written record proving Thomas's innocence, for instance.*

"Maybe so. Check that overstuffed storage room on the second floor. Listen, Mom, I've got to go. But I'll try to come down while you guys are still filming. It's too exciting to miss."

"If you can do it without skipping classes." Maggie gave Emily the expected mom response, but inwardly her heart sang. Every moment she spent with her daughter was precious.

"Don't worry—I'll get to all of my classes. Love you."

"Love you too." Maggie disconnected, then reached for the portrait. Her conversation with Emily had made up her mind. "You're coming downstairs with me. If your husband and I have to be in a video shoot, so do you."

. . . .

Maggie and James weren't the only ones who had decided to enjoy the fish-and-chips special. The barroom tucked inside the elegant Oceanview Hotel was jammed with customers, their chatter mingling with sports shows broadcasting from wall-mounted televisions.

"There's an empty table." Ushering Maggie along, James guided her to a two-top table next to the fireplace—and near the round table where Benton, Harry, Addison, and another man sat.

Benton spotted Maggie and James immediately, rising to greet them. He took Maggie's hand in both of his. "Have you fully recovered from your ordeal this afternoon?"

"Yes, thank you." Maggie remembered the message that had come in while she was on the boat. "I've heard from my attorney, and everything is all set with the contract. I'll do the show."

"Good to hear." Benton steered her and James toward his table. "I'd like you to meet Gene Percival, the new captain of the *Deep Six*. Gene, this is Maggie Watson, a descendant of Thomas Sedgwick, owner of the *Abigail*."

The captain was a bald, roly-poly man with a huge belly that strained the turtleneck under his blazer. "Hello, darlin'," he greeted her, his Southern accent even thicker than Benton's. "You didn't tell me you had such a fine filly involved with the project, Benton."

Maggie felt heat rise to her cheeks. "That's because I wasn't involved until just now."

Captain Gene guffawed, making his belly shake. "That's what I like—a girl with spirit."

James stepped forward, hand extended. "I'm James Bennett, Somerset Harbor alderman."

The captain shook his hand. "Ah, the local government. Guess we'd better watch our p's and q's. Might get our operation shut down." He gave another belly laugh.

Benton gave them a pained smile. "As you can see, our captain's a bit of a joker." He gestured toward two empty seats at their table. "Would you like to join us? We haven't eaten dinner yet."

Maggie wanted desperately to say no, but she couldn't think of a way to refuse gracefully. Then she glanced over her shoulder and noticed their table was gone, taken by another couple. "Shall we, James?" She nodded toward their now-filled seats.

"I guess we'd better." He helped her into a chair between Benton and Harry while he sat across the table between Addison and Gene.

"Here for the fish special?" Harry asked.

"We are," James said. He glanced around the table at the beer mugs sitting in front of everyone. "What's everyone drinking?"

"English ale." Addison raised his mug in salute. "Good with fish and chips."

"What can I get for you, Maggie?" James asked.

"An iced tea would be great." James went up to the bar to order. Seeing that Benton was engaged in discussion with Gene and Addison, Maggie turned to Harry. "I'm surprised to see you here," she whispered.

"Because of what happened earlier?" Harry gave a rueful shrug. "The man made me an offer I couldn't refuse. I'll be helping with weather forecasting and navigation."

"Aren't you still pulling traps?" Maggie knew that fall was a busy season for lobstermen.

"I only go out three days a week. So I'll be working for Benton some afternoons and evenings plus full days." He lowered his voice even further. "Money's good, and it allows me to keep an eye on what's happening with the salvage operation."

"I think a lot of people in town would love a chance to be involved." *Ina for one*, Maggie thought with amusement.

James returned with the drinks, followed by the waitress lugging platters of fish and chips. Everyone dug in after slathering the food with ketchup, tartar sauce, malt vinegar, and salt to their individual tastes.

"So you've recently joined the project?" James asked Gene.

"That's right. I usually work out of Miami, but when Addison here called sayin' I was needed, I flew up to Boston." Gene loaded his fork with chips and fish, somehow managing to wedge it all into his mouth.

"Our regular captain was injured," Benton said, "and we had to find someone fast so we could stay on schedule."

Gene wagged a thick finger. "Gotta keep the network happy. Wouldn't want them to pull the plug."

"I'm sorry to hear about your captain. What happened?" Maggie asked.

"He was mugged in an alley down at the docks." Benton shook his head. "Unfortunately he's still in the hospital."

"If that wasn't bad enough," Addison said, "we'd lost all our sailors for one reason or another. So we were really in a bind."

Maggie remembered hearing about one of the crew getting into a car accident.

"And don't forget, the engine was actin' up too." Gene shook his head. "Not to speak ill of your former captain, but that thing was a mess. I worked all night to get it right."

"Wow," James said. "That's a lot of bad luck." Glancing at Maggie, he raised his brows.

She swallowed a giggle, sensing that he was thinking about their earlier encounter with Clem. *Jinxed indeed.* It reminded her of the supposed curse of the pharaohs, which warned that those who dared to disturb their tombs would face death.

"Yep, it's a good thing they brought me on board, darlin'." Gene winked at Maggie. "If I had my guess, I'd say we could chalk up all the bad luck these fellas have had to the fact that certain rules of the sea were ignored, like allowing women on board." He shot a smug look at the men around the table. "But I'm getting everything straightened out." He threw a meaty elbow into Benton's side. "Including this guy." He brayed his raucous horselaugh again.

Addison joined in Gene's amusement, but Benton winced and ducked his head, his face flushed with anger. Maggie had the feeling he was barely tolerating the new captain.

"When do you need me for filming?" Maggie asked, more for a change of subject than out of eagerness, since she was still nervous about being on the show.

Benton raised his head. "I know it's short notice, but how about late tomorrow morning? I'd like to film a segment at the manor. Addison will interview you about your family."

Maggie gulped. "Tomorrow? That *is* soon." Her mind raced. How would she ever get the house, let alone herself, ready by then?

Benton tipped his glass toward Harry. "According to our weatherman, seas will be rough tomorrow morning. So we'll be docked."

Gene shook his head in mock amazement. "Gosh dawg, Miss Maggie, you're a brave one to air your family skeletons on national television." He glanced around the room. "Of course if we weren't in the middle of Yankee country, old Thomas Sedgwick might be somethin' to brag on."

Maggie leaned back in her chair, wanting nothing more than to escape this obnoxious man. "The man who built my home was not a Confederate sympathizer or a bank robber."

"Keep on tellin' yourself that, darlin'." With a grunt, Gene pushed back from the table. "Excuse me, I've gotta hit the little boys' room."

As Maggie watched him totter away, she was tempted to yell out, "And don't call me darlin'!" but she refrained.

Addison stood, holding his mug. "I'm headed for a refill. Anyone else?" They all shook their heads.

Once Addison was out of earshot, Benton said, "I must apologize for that oaf of a captain. If we hadn't been in a tight situation, I wouldn't have hired him. Of course, Addison says he knows his business, and that's what counts."

"He also seems to think he knows everyone else's," James said drily.

Harry grunted.

James glanced at Maggie's almost-empty plate. "Are you all set, Maggie? Maybe we should get going."

Maggie resisted the temptation to nibble on her last few French fries, thinking of being on camera. She supposed it was much too late to try to lose that pesky five pounds, but at least she could avoid making it worse. "Yes, I am. No dessert for me tonight." She turned to Benton. "See you tomorrow?"

"It will be Addison and the camera crew tomorrow, I'm afraid. I've got to go over Spot's approach plan with the techs."

Spot was the retrieval robot, Maggie remembered. "That sounds exciting. Are you going out to the site soon?"

"The minute my weatherman gives me the thumbs-up." Benton beamed at Harry. "Oh, and don't worry about the check," he told James. "I've added your meals to my bill."

"That was generous, but so much for taking you out for a

nice, relaxing dinner," James grumbled once they had their coats on and were trudging through the hotel lobby.

"You'll just have to take me out again." Maggie smiled up at him. "A do-over."

"Yes, one without the peanut gallery."

As James pulled into the manor drive, Maggie said, "I really appreciate you trying to end this stressful day on a pleasant note. What an experience it's been."

James grinned at her. "*Trying* might be the operative word, but I'm happy to do it." He pulled the Mercedes to a stop. "Wait there." He got out and walked around to open her door.

"Thanks," she said as she stepped out of the car. His chivalrous touches were nice, and she enjoyed them. "I'll see you soon."

She headed up the path to the front door, eyes on her purse as she dug out her house keys. When she looked up, her gaze was caught by something amiss.

A skeleton wearing a captain's hat was propped against the door.

6

Maggie screamed. James had apparently seen it from his car, as he'd already shut off the engine and was running toward her.

"Maggie, what is that?" He bounded up the porch steps.

"I seem to have a visitor," she said, trying to keep her voice steady. "From his appearance, I'd say he's been waiting quite a while." A bubble of hysterical laughter rose in her chest, and she forced it back down.

James recoiled. "That's gruesome." He bent to examine the skeleton. "Who would do such a thing?"

"I have no idea. It has to be a prank." *Or a warning.*

James suddenly paused in his examination. "Maggie, take a look at this."

She squatted down beside him and saw, clutched in the skeleton's left hand, a small drawstring bag, the neck open and folded back to reveal . . .

"Confederate gold," Maggie said in a stunned whisper. She stood and nudged the drawstring bag with the toe of her shoe, hearing the click of the plastic pieces inside as she jostled them against each other.

"It's blocking the front door." James reached out to grab the skeleton.

"Wait. Let me take a photograph first." Maggie rooted around in her bag for her phone. Finding it, she put the camera on night setting.

James folded his arms across his chest. "I think you should call the police."

Maggie held up the phone and took a photo. "I will in a

minute. It's not especially threatening, is it? Just rude." Had Abigail faced similar harassment after the shipwreck? She snapped another shot. "Probably someone saw the news and thought it would be funny to give me a scare."

"I don't think it's funny at all." James stepped forward and shifted the creepy gift to one side of the door.

"If this gets out, it will certainly give Clem fodder for his jinx theory," Maggie said as she dialed Robert Linton directly. She had worked with him often enough to know that he would answer her calls any time of day or night.

"Maggie. What's up?" Robert sounded alert despite the hour. In the background, Maggie heard the muted sounds of a sports broadcast.

"Sorry to bother you so late. James Bennett and I just got back to Sedgwick Manor from dinner to find a skeleton sitting at my front door. Wearing a captain's hat."

"Creepy. Do you need me to come over?"

"Only if you think you should. James thought it was important to make a report in case other things happen."

"Good point. Can it wait until morning?"

"Of course," Maggie said. "See you then." After she hung up, she turned to James. "Want a hot drink? I could use something to settle my nerves after this little incident."

"I'd love one." He pointed at the skeletal captain. "Think I should move him inside? I wouldn't want him to disappear before Robert sees him."

"That's probably best." She cocked her head. "Why are we calling it 'him'?"

"Beats me. The hat maybe?"

James carried the skeleton inside and set him down next to the hall table. Snickers came running and sniffed the object all over. Then he pulled back with what Maggie interpreted as a look of distaste. They both laughed. "I feel the same way, Snickers," she told him.

After hanging their coats, Maggie led the way to the kitchen, followed by James and Snickers. "I was tired earlier, but I have to admit, seeing that skeleton woke me right up." She opened the cupboard. "Would you like decaf coffee or herbal tea?"

"Decaf for me, thanks. Tea isn't my cup of tea after a night like we've had." He chuckled, and Maggie joined him.

"I'll have tea, because it's always my cup of tea." Maggie retrieved pods from the cupboard and popped his in the single-serve maker she used when making a small amount. Then she bent to add a little kibble to the cat's dish. "You don't need to diet, Snickers, but I wish I had time to. I'm going to be on television in a few hours."

James leaned against the counter, crossing his arms. "You look great, Maggie. Don't worry about it."

"Thanks for saying that, but I'm nervous." She glanced at the kitchen clock. Five minutes until nine. "Do you mind if I make a quick call to June? I'll need her help tomorrow morning."

"Go ahead. I'll fix my coffee." James opened the fridge to find milk.

Happy that he was so comfortable in her home, Maggie used the house phone to call June. "Pick up, please pick up," she whispered as it rang, praying she wasn't disturbing June in bed. She had little more than twelve hours to get the house—and herself—ready for her television debut.

* * * * * * * * * * * * * * * *

Despite the supposedly slumber-inducing tea blend, Maggie had a restless night. When she rose at six and glimpsed the bags under her eyes, she almost screamed. *Thank goodness for makeup.* She started the shower.

As she got out of the shower, the doorbell rang. She threw on a robe and hurried to the front door. Daisy, June, and Ina all stood on the porch as promised.

"We're your pit crew," Daisy said. "Here to help you with your television appearance." She hotfooted it into the house, carrying a paper sack and a tray of tall paper cups that emitted the inviting fragrance of coffee.

Then Daisy spotted the skeleton and stopped dead, forcing June and Ina to make detours around her. "What is *that*?"

June gave a little shriek, but Ina darted forward to inspect the bones.

"Bit early for Halloween, isn't it, Maggie?" Ina straightened the hat. "Nice touch. Captain Sedgwick?"

"I think so," Maggie said. "Someone left it on the porch for me last night."

"Ugh." June shuddered. "That must have been awful."

Daisy averted her eyes. "Now that I've lost a year of my life, let's get going on your makeup. We don't have much time."

"While Daisy works on you," June said, slipping off her jacket, "Ina and I are going to do a bit of straightening and cleaning around the house."

"That's right," Ina said. "After coffee, I'll vacuum." The older woman wore a ball cap that read PA.

"Pennsylvania?" Maggie asked, pointing at the hat.

"Nope. Production assistant." Ina pushed up the sleeves of her sweatshirt. "Where are they filming?"

"I think the library. Thomas Sedgwick's portrait is there, and last night, James and I rehung the portrait of Abigail next to it. Emily had commandeered it while she was home. Plus, the library is nicely furnished and intimate." Maggie had given the setting some thought. Although the living room was stunning, it was cavernous, and recorded sound might echo.

Ina nodded. "Good pick. I'll set out our breakfast."

June followed Maggie to the bedroom suite. "Have you decided what to wear?"

Maggie opened the door of the walk-in closet and stood there, paralyzed by the idea of choosing an outfit to wear on national television. All she could do was stare at the racks of clothes and shake her head.

June pushed past Maggie into the closet. "I read up on what to wear on television. You want a skirt suit in a flattering color, not black, red, or a print. Certainly not stripes." She leafed through the hangers and selected a tailored taupe jacket and skirt. "How about this? It will look good in the library against the background of the furniture and bookcases." She selected a brown silk button-up blouse to go with the suit. "This color looks great with your blonde hair."

Daisy entered the room, carrying a cosmetics case and a tote. "Go eat breakfast, and then I'll do your face and hair before you get dressed. Good thing that blouse doesn't have to go over your head."

"Yes ma'am." Maggie eyed her friend, who always sported elaborate hairdos and flattering makeup. "I'm so glad you're going to fix me up." She patted her cheeks. "I need help—a lot of it."

"Cut it out. You're gorgeous." Daisy placed her belongings next to the dressing table. "Now scoot." She began to set out hair implements and cosmetics.

In the kitchen, Maggie nibbled on a scone and tried to drink a cup of coffee, her stomach churning. Benton had sent a text saying the film crew would arrive at nine to set up. The minutes left before her television appearance were ticking away fast. How did people do this for a living? She would die from the jitters within a week. Of course, one advantage was that she wouldn't be able to eat, if this morning was any indication. Her stubborn five pounds would be history.

The ringing of the doorbell interrupted her musings. Fortunately, Ina ran to get it. "My nephew is here to see Mr. Bones," she said, dashing back into the kitchen.

Maggie put aside her crumbled scone and hurried out to the hall. She really didn't need to deal with this right now. Fortunately she was able to send Robert on his way quickly, the skeleton riding in the cruiser, and then she submitted herself to Daisy's expertise.

Within half an hour she didn't recognize herself. No circles under her eyes now; instead she had long lashes and flawless skin. Her gleaming hair bounced.

"Wow, Daisy, can you do that to me?" June asked.

"Of course." Daisy started putting the tools of her trade into her tote. "Nothing I like more than dolling up my beautiful friends."

"I'll be needing you again," Maggie said, "if they want to film me more than once."

Ina popped into the room. "The film crew is here. Shall I tell them to set up in the library?"

"Please, Ina. Thanks." Maggie rose from the dressing table bench. "I'd better get dressed and hurry out there."

"I'll make fresh coffee and put out some of those scones in the dining room," June said, "in case the crew would like a snack."

The crew consisted of a camera operator and a light-and-audio technician; Maggie greeted them when she entered the library.

"Hi, I'm Kristen," the woman setting up standing lights said. Dressed in jeans and a T-shirt, she wore her dark hair in a ponytail. "And that's Chris."

"Kristen and Chris. That should be easy to remember. I'm Maggie Watson."

The man raising a tripod waved. "Nice to meet you. I hope this setup is okay. I'm putting you and Addison in front of the fireplace in those wingback chairs." He bent to unlatch a camera case.

"That's perfect." Maggie wandered over to gaze up at the portrait of Thomas Sedgwick. What would he think if he knew his life had become the subject of national interest? She moved to touch the frame holding Abigail's portrait. What had she felt and thought about everything that had happened? Seeing the picture reminded Maggie that she needed to dig into the storage room and see if she could find anything belonging to Abigail after the shoot.

Her stomach swooping with nerves, Maggie took a deep breath and turned to watch the crew. Kristen had finished with the lights and was now fiddling with microphones.

The doorbell rang again, and Maggie heard Addison's deep drawl out in the hall. He strode into the library, Ina at his heels. Today he wore a casual suit jacket and tie, the way Richard had often dressed for college functions.

"Good. You're almost ready," Addison said after the exchange of greetings. He crossed the room to stand beside Maggie while Ina hovered around the crew, asking questions. "I assume this is our space?"

"Yes. I thought it was more intimate than the living room."

Addison's gaze landed on the picture of Abigail. "This must be Abigail Sedgwick. Pretty woman, but I guess still waters run deep." A knowing expression flitted across his face as he gave the gilt frame a tap.

"What do you mean?" Again Maggie wondered what the professor knew. He seemed so certain of Thomas's guilt.

"All in good time, Maggie, all in good time." Turning, Addison clasped his hands behind his back in a professorial posture. "It looks like we'll be ready to roll in a few. I'd love a cup of coffee if you have one."

"In the dining room. We have scones too."

Addison patted his trim waist. "Thanks, but none for me. The camera adds ten pounds, you know."

Maggie smoothed her jacket, thankful it skimmed over her hips. *Great. Not only am I carrying an extra five, but the camera will make it look like fifteen!*

Kristen smiled at her. "Don't worry about it. We know what we're doing. You'll look great."

"I guess you read my mind."

The young woman nodded. "Everyone worries about looking fat on camera. That's why everyone in LA is a size zero."

Chris looked at her. "Remember the Caribbean wreck when Benton's wife was on the show? She wanted to review all the footage after and make us do retakes."

Kristen's eyes narrowed. "You mean his ex-wife. And yes I do. She made my life miserable."

"Yeah, she said the lights made her look old." Chris shook his head. "Poor you."

Maggie put her hands to her cheeks. Compared to these kids, she *was* old. She would be so glad when this ordeal was over. She vowed never to watch herself on-screen. She didn't want to know.

And if Meredith was Benton's ex-wife as Kristen had said, why had she followed him to Somerset Harbor?

All too soon—but also not soon enough—Chris pronounced the shoot ready to roll. Addison settled himself into one of the wingback chairs, legs crossed, and Maggie sat in the other. Hoping to minimize her midsection, she sat slightly sideways, knees and feet together, hands in her lap.

"Loosen up, Maggie," Chris said, peering through the viewfinder. "You're not on trial."

With a laugh, Maggie forced herself to relax. She fixed her eyes on Addison, hoping she looked intelligent and attractive.

Addison gave an introduction about the show, then said, "At the invitation of Ms. Maggie Watson, current resident, we're in the library of the magnificent Sedgwick Manor, built by Captain Thomas Sedgwick for his wife, Abigail. Like many of the wealthiest Maine residents of the time, Thomas was a sea captain. Right, Maggie?"

Maggie thought she detected an edge to Addison's tone, an insinuation, making it sound like there was something underhanded about the captain. "That's right, Professor. But the Sedgwicks' fortune was inherited. The captain was a naval officer. They invested in their community, supporting the church and worthy charities." That was something she'd learned from Liz Young, who had mentioned the long-standing tradition of Sedgwick gifts to the church.

Kristen was in Maggie's line of sight, and the technician gave her a subtle thumbs-up at Maggie's retort.

Addison recovered quickly and went on. "Thanks for sharing that tidbit of family history. That's a portrait of Thomas Sedgwick over the mantel, isn't it?" He rose to stand and gaze up at the painting. At a gesture from Kristen, Maggie joined him.

"Yes it is. A very nice portrait, although I always get the feeling his eyes are watching me, making sure I'm on my best behavior."

The professor laughed dutifully. "I sometimes think the artists painted them that way on purpose." He pointed to Abigail. "And this is a photograph of his wife, correct?"

"Yes it is. I don't think there are any other pictures of Abigail in existence. At that time, having photographs made was quite rare."

"About the time of the Civil War, correct?" At Maggie's assent, he turned to face the camera. "And that brings us to the subject of this episode of *Deep Sea Secrets*. As you know, we're preparing to salvage cargo from the *Abigail*, the ship captained by Thomas Sedgwick." His voice became a low, bewitching rumble. "A ship carrying Confederate gold."

"Cut," Chris said. "Sit down again, guys. You're both doing awesome."

"Wow, you're good," Maggie said, settling in her seat once again. "You're making the story sound thrilling, even if your version is inaccurate."

"Ouch." Chris winced. "She got you there, Professor. All right, are you ready?" He grinned. "You might want to wipe that glare off your face, Addison."

Addison smoothed out his expression with obvious effort. "Maggie, what was your reaction when you heard about the *Abigail* carrying Confederate gold?"

She put up a hand. "First let me clarify. The gold was actually stolen from a bank in Boston, so it wasn't lawfully Confederate gold." Kristen made a "you go, girl" face behind Addison's back. Maggie suppressed a smile. "As for my reaction, well, it was shock, of course."

"You hadn't heard the tale?"

"No, I only recently inherited the mansion from my aunt, and although I visited as a child, I'm not totally up-to-date regarding family history."

"You hadn't heard that Thomas Sedgwick loaded his boat with gold and was on his way to Canada with Confederate compatriots when the ship hit the rocks during a storm?"

Maggie felt heat rising in her face and wondered if her blush would show up on camera. Clasping her hands tightly in her lap, she said, "No, I hadn't heard that. And I don't believe—"

Addison interrupted her. "So I'm assuming you also don't know that Abigail Sedgwick provided lodging to a group of Confederate spies during the war." He leaned forward and leered at her. "I believe they call that treason."

7

Maggie's mind reeled. *What is Addison talking about? Abigail Sedgwick allowed rebel spies to stay here, in this house?*

"I'm afraid I have never heard that story. It sounds ridiculous." Maggie attempted a laugh, but even to her own ears, it sounded flat. She glanced over at the doorway to see her friends watching. All of them looked as stunned as she felt.

Addison smirked. "Not many people know about it. I put it together myself with information I found in historical society archives in South Carolina." He settled back in his chair, a hand propping his chin, one foot swinging in contentment. "You see, a band of spies infiltrated Maine, posing as—get this—*artists*. A letter from one of them referenced their visit to Somerset Harbor and the 'gracious Mrs. Sedgwick, who kindly provided us lodging and a meal.'"

For a long moment, Maggie didn't know what to say. Then she rallied. "Isn't it true, Professor, that people often put interpretations on historical events that later turn out to be false?"

He stroked his chin. "That is true, I suppose. On occasion—"

This time she interrupted. "I intend to investigate Thomas and Abigail Sedgwick myself. I will clear their names. I refuse to believe that the captain robbed a bank and helped criminals escape, or that his wife knowingly entertained spies during wartime."

Kristen made a silent clapping motion, and risking a glance at her friends, Maggie saw they approved also.

Addison hoisted himself to his feet. "I wish you luck, dear lady. I do have to warn you, though, that as an amateur, you don't have access to the same resources I do. I have spent years researching this event." He turned to Chris. "Edit my last words out. But keep Maggie's." He grinned slyly down at Maggie. "Nothing like controversy and argument to boost ratings."

Great, on the backs of my family. Maggie was getting a taste of how unpleasant it was to be in the spotlight of tabloid attention. This was worse than she had imagined.

"Where are we headed after this, Addison?" Chris asked.

"To the *Deep Six*. We're going out to the site at two o'clock this afternoon." Addison turned to Maggie. "I hope you will join us. We're sending Spot down to explore the wreck for the gold."

"I wouldn't miss that for anything." Despite her annoyance with the professor, Maggie wanted to be there. Maybe the gold was nothing but a rumor. That would disappoint a lot of people, but she would be relieved.

"So it's the big reveal." Chris gave a thumbs-up. "The moment of truth."

Ina dashed into the room. "Can I go too? Maybe you need a PA."

Addison shook his head. "I'm afraid not. The set will be restricted. We have to keep what we retrieve under wraps until Benton decides to announce it."

"Darn it." Ina snapped her fingers in disappointment.

"I hope you find more than rotted wood and rusty metal." Kristen's eyes sparkled with mischief. "That wouldn't make for a very good story."

Addison shot her an irritated glare. "We will. I have absolutely no doubt of that."

"Let me show you out," Maggie said to Addison, hoping to speed him on his way. She'd had enough of his imputations for one day.

Once he was gone, she poured herself a cup of coffee and offered refreshments to Chris and Kristen to snack on while they took down their equipment. Daisy, June, and Ina also left after

Ina asked them to keep her in mind if she was needed.

"That Ina is a hoot," Chris said. "I like her spunk."

"Me too." Maggie took a sip of her coffee. "It must be fun working for Benton and traveling around to different shipwrecks."

"It's a good gig." Chris carefully set the camera in its case. "I'm a diver, and in my free time I get to explore some of the best waters in the world."

"Not the Maine coast, I'm guessing," Maggie said.

"You're right." Chris laughed. "Afraid it's not quite as appealing as the Caribbean."

"How do you like it, Kristen?"

The sound tech paused in the act of winding cords. "It's . . . okay." A strange expression crossed her face. She set the cords down. "Can I please use your powder room?"

"Of course." Maggie led the young woman to the doorway and pointed. "Down the hall past the stairs and to the right. First door on the left."

"Don't mind her," Chris said to Maggie after Kristen's footsteps died away. "She's having guy trouble. And before you ask, it's not me. Though not for lack of trying." He winked.

"Oh, a boyfriend back home? It must be difficult being away from her significant other for months at a time."

"Nope." Chris latched the case. "Someone in the company."

After the crew left, Maggie still had a couple of hours before she was due at the boat, so after making sure June was all right at the shop, she decided to head over to the library and see what information she could find about the Sedgwicks. Previous research projects had informed her that the local paper, *The Somerset Harbor Herald*, hadn't gone into production until the 1870s, after the Civil War, so she wouldn't try their archives. She made a mental note to check for other Maine papers from the time while at the library.

The day was warm with a slight breeze, so Maggie decided to walk. After shedding her suit, she slipped into more comfortable clothes—jeans, sneakers, a T-shirt, fleece, and a windbreaker. Layers, in case of temperature changes. Heating up as she walked down the hill, she took off her windbreaker and tied it around her waist.

Despite being tempted to stop at The Busy Bean, Maggie turned up Harbor Street instead. The library was located on the corner of Broad Street and Water Way, next to the post office. Maggie enjoyed walking the streets of Somerset Harbor's downtown, gazing at the brick and clapboard shops and restaurants. In addition to enjoying the architecture, being on foot gave her time to peruse window displays. The shoe store was one of her favorites, currently featuring to-die-for boots.

Had Abigail Sedgwick done the same? Or as the wife of a prominent captain, had she used a carriage? Or perhaps she'd had her purchases delivered? Somerset Harbor had been even smaller then, consisting of mostly wooden buildings. Maggie had seen some early photographs, both before and after a fire had ravaged the downtown. The blocks of brick buildings had been constructed afterward, grander and more impervious to weather and fire.

Maggie breathed deeply as she entered the Somerset Harbor Library, perhaps one of the oddest and most intriguing buildings in town. Two stories high, it looked like the hull of a ship, complete with portholes. Maggie always got a kick out of its funky architecture.

Librarian Maura O'Brien looked up from her station behind the front desk. "Good morning, Maggie. How can I help you?"

Maggie approached the desk. "Hi, Maura. I'm wondering if you have any microfiche for newspapers prior to the founding of the *Herald*."

Maura pursed her lips in thought. "Perhaps. What years are you looking for?"

"Between 1861 and 1864. The Civil War."

The librarian's eyes twinkled. "Are you researching Thomas Sedgwick by chance?" She leaned forward across the desk, lowering her voice as other patrons looked their way. "I heard about the treasure hunt. So exciting!"

It appeared that even the normally discreet librarian was on the treasure hunt bandwagon.

"Yes, I have to admit I am," Maggie said. "So were there any local newspapers in existence before the *Herald*?"

Maura shook her head as she came around the end of the counter. "I'm afraid not. However, I can tap you into the Maine State Library. They're fortunate enough to have access to digitized newspaper databases." She led the way to a bank of computers, most of them occupied, and settled Maggie at an empty one.

She handed Maggie a binder and showed her how to access the library catalog and from there, log into databases via university sites.

"This is fantastic," Maggie said. "When I lived in Bennington, I loved going to the college library. I didn't realize you could get into them this way."

"Yes, it connects little Somerset Harbor to the bigger world. You have one hour per session. Good luck." Maura swished away to the front desk, where someone was waiting to check out.

Maggie knew the date of the shipwreck—early morning on September 13, 1864—so she looked for newspapers published around that time. So many of the titles were no longer in existence, and some had quaint names, like the *Bangor Daily Whig and Courier*. Figuring that coverage of the shipwreck would include information about the bank robbery, she decided to search Boston papers first.

As she feared, the newspapers put the worst spin possible on events. *Maine Ship Carrying Stolen Gold Sinks. Captain Believed Connected to Rebel Plot.* Maggie's heart sank. It couldn't be clearer what people had thought about Thomas. Poor Abigail. It must have been horrible to see the newspapers and hear the whispers. Had people shunned her? No wonder she'd run away to a cabin to live.

Maggie skimmed the article, then sent it to her e-mail address so she could print it and study it in more detail later. The next few issues had follow-up articles, and she sent those along too.

When she checked her phone to make sure the e-mails had gone through to her account, she saw she had a new message from Addison Stringfellow. Curious, she opened it to find the picture of the *Abigail,* as promised. She tried to zoom in on it, but her phone's screen was too small to see it well. She'd have to try enlarging it on a computer.

Glancing at the clock, she saw an hour had flown by. She had barely enough time to grab a bite to eat at The Busy Bean, and then it would be time to board the ship. Her stomach clenched. *They might actually find gold today.*

Awhile later, as she walked down to the docks with Daisy, Maggie realized the *Deep Six* was easily the biggest ship in the harbor—over one hundred feet in length, she estimated. Antennas and cranes protruded from the roof and deck, giving it an industrial appearance. Seagulls circled the craft, squawking.

"Harry's already on board?" she asked Daisy.

"Yes. He said he'd bring the dinghy to the dock to pick us up." Daisy waved. "There he is now."

A small rubber boat buzzed away from the shelter of the larger ship, heading toward the floating docks where small boats were tied up. Maggie and Daisy hurried to join him.

"Are you excited about seeing what they dig up today, Maggie?" Harry asked as he helped her in.

"Yes and no. Of course finding gold is exciting, but I'm not happy about the theory that Thomas was involved in a crime." She sat down in the bow, facing Daisy, who sat in the middle seat, and Harry in the rear. As Harry started the outboard motor and pulled away, Maggie filled them in about the newspaper articles she had found. "So everyone believed that Thomas was in league with those bank robbers. Not only do they think he was a thief, but a traitor as well."

"I can see why that would bother a person," Harry said.

"Me too." Daisy patted Maggie's knee. "But try to remember that it is ancient history. And maybe you'll uncover something that proves he was simply in the wrong place at the wrong time."

"Exactly. Aunt Evelyn implied there was proof around. Now I just need to find it."

They quickly traversed the harbor and arrived at the rear of the *Deep Six*. As Harry secured the boat, Maggie stared up at the metal stern of the ship, looming like a huge wall, a winch boom hovering even higher above that. "How do we get up there?"

Harry pointed to a ladder attached to the side. "Up that."

"I was hoping you wouldn't say that." Maggie quailed at the idea of clambering up the ladder.

"It will be all right," Daisy said. "I'll go first, you follow, and Harry will be right behind you. Keep your eyes on me and don't look down. That will help."

"I'll catch you if you fall," Harry said.

Right before we go into the deep. Maggie took a deep breath and wiped her clammy hands on her pants. Then she grabbed the nearest rung and began to climb, keeping her eyes focused on Daisy all the way.

Captain Gene helped her over the railing with a chuckle. "You're lookin' a little peaked, Miss Maggie. I'm guessing ladders aren't your thing."

"They're not," Maggie said, wiping her hands on her jeans again.

He leaned close and whispered behind his hand. "Don't think too hard about going back down, then."

"Thanks a lot." Maggie glanced at the water far below. Now that was all she was going to think about until she was safely back in the dinghy.

Gene bellowed in amusement at her irritation. "Time's a-wastin', so come on. The team is waiting for you below." He guided Maggie and the Carters across a wide deck crammed with equipment—a crane attached to a contraption labeled Spot, metal containers, inflatable boats—and into a large room lined with windows and furnished with couches and chairs. On the far side, Gene opened a door and preceded them down a metal staircase. "The brains of the operation are down here," he explained, then tapped his head. "Not up here."

Maggie could practically feel Harry and Daisy's eyes rolling at the captain's corny wit.

A sign on the door read Command Center, and Gene tapped on it before entering. "Got the rest of the onlookers here, Benton. I'll be heading back up, then it's anchors aweigh." With a final chuckle, he lumbered out of the room.

"Thanks, Gene." Benton swiveled in his chair at a long L-shaped table and gestured to Maggie and the Carters. "Come on in." On the walls, a dozen or more computer monitors were mounted, each showing a different viewpoint.

Maggie saw that Chris and Kristen were set up in the opposite corner, camera and microphones trained on Benton, Rory, and two computer techs seated at the table. Addison stood nearby, hovering silently.

"Roll 'em, Chris," Benton said. "I want to film my introductory speech with Maggie."

Maggie put a hand to her chest. "Really? I didn't expect that." Good thing she hadn't washed off the face paint Daisy had applied hours earlier.

Benton beckoned to her. "You'll be fine. Don't worry, I'll do all the talking."

"That's right, mate," Rory said. "We all know that." He rolled his eyes.

Everyone laughed, a little dutifully to Maggie's ears. She moved to join Benton at the table, feeling the vibration of engines under her feet as she did so. They must be under way.

"Welcome to the *Deep Six*, Maggie," Benton said.

He paused, so she said, "I'm glad to be here. This is exciting." A thrill of nerves ran down her spine. Maybe she would get used to being filmed after all. "I can't wait to explore the *Abigail*—from the surface, that is."

The others laughed again, this time sounding more genuine.

"That's a perfect segue," Benton said. "Technology allows us to do everything from the safety and comfort of this cabin. In the old days, people risked their lives to explore shipwrecks." He pointed to an old-fashioned diving helmet on a shelf. "Can you imagine going down into dark, deep, murky water wearing that thing?"

Maggie shuddered. "I can't imagine doing that for any reason."

"Not even for gold?"

She shook her head firmly. "Not even for gold." As she turned away from the helmet, her gaze fell on Kristen, who was staring in their direction. She was surprised by the dreamy look she saw in the girl's eyes. Could Benton be the mysterious significant other Chris had mentioned, especially since, apparently, he wasn't married after all? Except for the techs and Chris, the other men in the room were easily twice Kristen's age. *Ugh.*

Benton's voice pulled her attention from the young woman. "Well, you're in luck, Maggie. We don't need those dangerous ancient methods any longer. Eric, tell us how we find the exact location of shipwrecks."

A technician tapped on his keyboard, and sonar maps of the seabed appeared on one of the large monitors. "Last year we ran lines in this area with a sonar fish, creating a grid. We also took high-resolution photographs of any area where we saw anomalies, indications that parts of a ship were resting on the bottom." He brought up a photograph on the screen. "Before." He clicked and a different photograph appeared. "And after."

"Those pictures are made up of numerous photographs put together in a composite," Benton said. "Can you see the ship's hull?"

"I sure can," Maggie said. The colorization they used had transformed otherwise meaningless shapes into the unmistakable outline of a ship, with its pointed prow and squared-off stern. How amazing that technology was allowing them to closely examine a ship lost over a century ago!

"Today we're sending our retriever, Spot, down for some other objects that look interesting." Rory nodded and the tech brought up another photograph that resembled small lumps on the bottom. "We think that might be the gold."

"I know it is." Addison crossed his arms, frowning. "Everything I've learned points to that wreck being the *Abigail*."

"And the professor is always right." Rory gave him a mock salute.

"We'll find out soon." Benton glanced at his watch. "We should be at the site in a few minutes. Let's break for coffee while we wait."

Finally the *Deep Six* was situated over the wreck, a dynamic positioning system keeping them in place, as Benton explained to Maggie. Up on deck, they watched as an operator jumped into the booth to operate the on-deck crane that controlled Spot. He pushed levers, making the crane arm lift the rectangular device, about the size of a two-ton truck, several feet up in the air.

Then it stalled, to the groans and disappointed cries of the onlookers. "We've been having trouble with the hydraulics," Rory told Maggie. Benton spoke into a radio, telling the machine operator to lower the device. Benton went around to the other side of the crane with another member of the crew.

Radios crackled, and the operator threw levers again. The crane whined, then Spot rose into the air, dangled for a moment, and swung out over the rail. The crewman who had been with Benton came running, arms waving. "Stop! Stop! Benton is caught on the device!" he shouted to Rory.

Maggie and the others ran to the railing. To her shock, she saw Benton clinging to Spot's side, his legs dangling twenty feet above the treacherous ocean.

8

Rory ran toward the operator in his booth, who didn't seem to know what was going on. The crane jerked and Benton was jolted sideways, legs swinging.

Daisy screamed.

Could Benton hang on or would he fall? Maggie grabbed Harry's arm. "What can we do?"

"Not much." Harry glared at the operator. "He needs to get Benton back on board and fast. I'm going to find out what the problem is." With a huff of disgust, he trotted away to join Rory, who was pointing and gesturing. The operator tapped his headset in response, shaking his head.

Finally, when it seemed that Benton would surely lose his grip and fall, the mechanical arm began to turn slowly again. Benton cleared the rail and was gently set down on the deck. Daisy ran to his side, followed by Maggie.

"Benton, are you all right?" Daisy asked.

He leaned over, propping his hands on his knees, breathing deeply. "I'll be okay in a minute. That scared the pants off me." Straightening, he rolled one shoulder then the other. "Excuse me, ladies, I need to go find out what happened."

The cameraman had followed them outside and was using a handheld camera.

"You're going to use this in the show?" Maggie asked.

Chris paused his filming. "Absolutely. Disasters and screw-ups add drama. My job is to capture everything." He cocked an eyebrow toward Kristen, who was standing nearby. She pulled a face at his comment. "Well, almost everything." He aimed the camera at the cluster of men arguing by the crane booth.

A few minutes later, they broke up and the crane began to whine again. "We're back on schedule," Rory called. "Going for the gold." He pumped a fist to cheers while Chris zoomed in.

This time Spot was lifted off the deck and lowered into the ocean without incident. After the device vanished under the waves, the group went back inside to watch its video feed.

Maggie shifted from foot to foot as she watched Spot's camera search the ocean floor. Thanks to the spotlight, it looked as bright as day. Still, it was difficult to identify specific objects on the muddy and rocky bottom. Kind of like reading an ultrasound—only trained technicians knew how to recognize parts of a baby.

"See that?" Benton pointed to a long, cylindrical object. "That's a cannon. Most merchant ships carried them, especially during wartime."

"If Thomas's ship was armed, how could the Confederates take over?" Maggie asked.

"Because he welcomed them aboard," Addison simpered.

Maggie flushed with annoyance at Addison's habit of debating with her. "Say he didn't. How would that have happened?"

"It could be that he was docked in Boston Harbor," Rory said. "They might have hidden in the hold until he was under way—out of reach of help from shore—and taken over then. The cannon would be useless in that case."

Maggie imagined the bandits swarming up from below and overpowering the captain and his mates. "That does sound plausible, Rory."

"There's what we think may be coins," Benton said as the wandering light reached a heap of small, circular, muddy objects. "Focus in."

The tech obeyed, zooming the camera in. Then he maneuvered

the articulating arm to vacuum up several piles of the objects. "How's that, Benton?"

"Good. Bring it back up. Let's see what we have."

Back up on deck, Spot sat glistening in the weak September sun. Its silted, sandy load was disgorged into a plastic basin with a swirl of seawater. Rory, holding the pan, hooted. "I'm panning for gold, folks." He shifted the pan back and forth, making the contents jostle.

"Be careful with that." Addison stepped forward, hands out toward Rory. "No matter what it is, it's still archeological salvage and of great historical value."

"Yes, boss." Rory began to walk gingerly across the deck. "I'm taking this to the laboratory," he said into the camera. "There we will learn exactly what these are."

Only Benton, Rory, Addison, and Maggie were allowed into the laboratory. After Benton closed the door, he said, "We're at a delicate junction, team. No one outside this room must know the results of our test. Once we salvage all the gold, then yes. Otherwise we'll get a deluge of treasure ships from around the globe tonight."

"That must be a problem with all your sites," Maggie said.

"It is." Rory set the pan on a long counter. "But the exact coordinates of most are unknown, except to us. That isn't true for the *Abigail*."

Watching Benton carefully rinse what appeared to be coins in soapy water, Maggie had a thought. "How did anyone know for certain the *Abigail* was here, near Deadmen's Shoals? I thought there were no survivors."

"As far as we know, there weren't." Addison leaned against the counter, watching Rory closely. "Probably someone local figured it out from where wreckage washed up."

"I'm guessing it wasn't the first ship to be lost here." Maggie was fascinated to see a dull gold gleam emerging from the murk.

"No, we've found remains of several others," Benton said. "But they were much smaller. Probably local fishing boats." Wearing gloves, he placed the coins on a soft cloth, then pulled one from its fellows for closer examination. First he measured the coin to determine diameter and thickness. Then he studied it with a high-powered magnifying glass.

"What do we have, mate?" Rory fairly vibrated with eagerness and nerves.

Lowering the magnifying glass, Benton smiled with satisfaction. "What would y'all say to a perfect 1860 Liberty Head twenty-dollar piece?"

Addison's gaze sharpened. "Which mint? Philadelphia?"

Benton chuckled. "No sir. By some miracle, it says *O*." He set the coin down on the cloth and fished another out of the pile.

Rory slapped his forehead. "I can't believe it." He wavered, then sat down hard on a stool.

"What does that mean?" Maggie asked.

Blinking furiously, Addison took off his glasses and wiped them with a soft cloth. "It means the coin was struck at the New Orleans mint, which happened to be closed during the Civil War. So finding one in an 1864 shipment is unusual." He paused to settle his glasses back on his nose. "At the lowest, it's worth about double a Philadelphia coin, and depending on condition, it could be worth as much as $100,000."

Maggie's belly hollowed in shock. "How many coins were on the ship?" *If they were all rare . . .* Her mind boggled before she finished the thought.

"We don't know for certain," Benton said. "But about $200,000 was taken, most of it in gold." He held up the second coin. "Even if only a portion of the haul is the quality of these, the cargo is worth far more than we estimated. Maybe tens of millions."

. . . .

When the boat docked and Harry returned her to shore, Maggie trudged home, not caring that a shower had blown in and rain was trickling down her neck and soaking her face and hair. They had found the *Abigail's* gold. And not only that, the coins might be rare and incredibly valuable. The worst thing about it was that she couldn't tell a soul.

A confidentiality agreement was part of her contract, and she had assumed it was so she wouldn't spill details of the show. Now she had an extraordinary secret lodged in her belly like a volcano about to erupt.

She couldn't tell anyone. Not even the other members of the historical society or her daughter. Or James. How she wished she could confide in him! He always had wise advice to offer.

At home, Snickers greeted her with plaintive mews alleging neglect. After removing her dripping windbreaker and soggy sneakers, she hunkered down to pat him. "Can I tell you my secret, Snickers?"

In response, he brushed against her knee, purring loudly. Then he butted her with his head, one of his signals that he wanted a treat.

Amused, she straightened and padded to the kitchen to refill his kibble dish. Then she hurried to the bedroom, eager to take a shower and warm up. She was rinsing her hair when she suddenly remembered something. It was odd how ideas often came to her while showering, walking, or doing dishes. She suspected it must be due to the mindless peace of the activities.

A section of Evelyn's journal was devoted to family heirlooms, most of which were stuffed in the second-floor storeroom. Emily had given her the idea that there could be something of Abigail's in that room that would shed light on the shipwreck.

After pulling on toasty wool socks, comfy yoga pants, and a cotton top, Maggie went to the office to look at the journal. Outside the tall window, rain streamed down, making her feel extra cozy sitting in the leather chair behind the flame mahogany partners desk in the manor's office. Snickers followed her, jumping up onto a brocade-upholstered Queen Anne chair and curling up.

Opening the journal reminded Maggie that she still hadn't found the figurehead. She needed to see if she could get some details from the photograph so she and June could find it, either in the mansion or the shop. She would do that next.

She turned to the section labeled *Secrets and Mysteries: Second-Floor Storage Room*, smiling at the drama of Aunt Evelyn's words. Abigail Sedgwick's story certainly fit those categories. Scanning the pages quickly for any mention of her ancestor, Maggie finally spotted something that made her heart leap.

One small brass-bound trunk containing household papers left by Abigail Sedgwick.

There was even a quote, as Evelyn was inclined to provide, this one from Pericles:

"Just because you do not take an interest in politics doesn't mean politics won't take an interest in you."

Regarding the tragic fate of the Sedgwicks, no truer words were ever spoken. Despite the circumstantial evidence of gold aboard the *Abigail*, Maggie staunchly believed that Thomas Sedgwick had been a mere pawn, a victim. Addison's words echoed in her mind: *Abigail Sedgwick provided lodging to a group of Confederate spies.*

If so, then it was inadvertent. Maggie was sure of it. Taking her courage in both hands, she stood. "I'm going to learn the truth, no matter what it is," she told Snickers. He opened one eye, the one not covered by his tail, making her laugh. "Coming with me?"

Upstairs, Maggie slipped into the storeroom, flicking on the overhead light so she could see. So much stuff crammed the space that it blocked the windows, making the room dim even in the daytime. Snickers wove past her feet and went to his favorite place in the room—a tiny patch of carpet.

"Brass-bound trunk, brass-bound trunk," Maggie muttered to herself as she sidled past a wardrobe, a rack holding garment bags, stacked chairs, and a pile of cardboard boxes. Even the idea of sorting through those was daunting.

A trunk that fit the description was tucked in a corner, behind a maple drop leaf table. Maggie had just wedged herself into the small space between a bureau and the table when the doorbell rang. Her first thought was to ignore it since she wasn't expecting anyone. But the chime came again, this time longer and more insistent. What if it was important, like Robert Linton with some information about the skeleton? She patted her pants before realizing she didn't have any pockets, which meant her phone was downstairs. No one could reach her, and maybe someone had resorted to coming in person.

With a grumbling sigh, she backed out of the corner and inched through the storeroom to the hall. As the bell rang a third time, she flew down the stairs and crossed the foyer to the front door.

Television personality Stella Marquez stood on the porch, an amused smile on her pretty features. "Did I catch you at a bad time?" She wore a belted trench coat and carried an open plaid umbrella.

Maggie brushed at her hair and removed a dust bunny. *Yes.* "No. I was upstairs looking through the storeroom." She opened the door wider. "Would you like to come in?" As she issued the automatic invitation, her thoughts were still upstairs with that trunk. She was dying to see what was inside.

Stella folded her umbrella, staring curiously around the foyer and into the open doors to the left and right. "What a gorgeous old house. Nineteenth century, correct?"

"That's right." Maggie hung up Stella's coat and plopped her umbrella into the stand. "Would you like tea or coffee?"

"Tea sounds wonderful on a day like this." Stella peered around as she followed Maggie back to the kitchen, making little squeals of excitement when she spotted details she liked.

In the kitchen, Maggie put the kettle on while Stella burbled about the grand living room, the magnificent staircase, the stunning crystal chandelier. "Oh, and that library is to die for. Floor-to-ceiling bookcases and a rolling ladder?" Stella laid a hand on her chest. "I'm smitten."

"It's one of my favorite rooms. In fact, that's where we filmed a segment for the reality show today." As soon as she'd said it, Maggie wished she could take back the words. Trying to hide her discomfort, she opened the fridge and began to rummage. "Do you take lemon or milk?"

"Milk, please." Like a hound scenting prey, Stella fixed on her main target. "Benton and his crew filmed here? Then you absolutely *have* to let me do a feature too." Her voice softened, a wheedling tone creeping in. "You promised to think about it, remember?"

With a start of guilt, Maggie belatedly remembered saying that at the shop to put the reporter off. Since then she hadn't given Stella or *Seacoast Today* another thought.

"I'm sorry. It's been so hectic." Maggie placed a basket of tea packets in front of Stella, sitting in the breakfast nook. "Pick out whichever one you want."

Stella leafed through the tea bags, considering one then another. Handing one to Maggie, she glanced up. "Exciting news today, wasn't it?"

"How did—" Maggie bit off the rest of the sentence but not before the reporter's eyes lit up with delight.

"So you *did* find something out there." Stella sat back, pushing the basket away. "Was it gold?"

The reporter had set a trap, and Maggie had fallen right in like a naïve fool. Without answering, she hurried to move the shrieking kettle from the heat. She tore Stella's tea packet open and placed the tea bag in a mug, then drowned it in boiling water. She served the tea to Stella along with a pitcher of milk. "Do you need sugar?"

Stella patted the table. "Maggie, sit." After Maggie collapsed on the bench beside the reporter, she said, "That wasn't fair of me. I'm sorry."

"No it wasn't." Maggie squeezed her hands together in her lap. "But I'm not admitting to a thing." She shook her head. "I can't. I'm bound by an agreement." Panic thrummed in her temples. If word got out and ruined Benton's expedition, he stood to lose millions.

And it would be all her fault.

9

Stella put a hand on Maggie's arm, making her jump. "I won't say a word to anyone. After all, you really didn't tell me anything, did you?"

Maggie's racing heart began to slow. Maybe Stella would give her a reprieve. But she couldn't figure out the woman's motivation. Wasn't breaking juicy stories the lifeblood of Stella's career?

"Make yourself a cup of tea and we'll talk," Stella said.

Going through the motions, Maggie did as Stella suggested, choosing a spicy chai she enjoyed. She brought her mug to the table. "Okay, shoot."

Stella sighed, running a hand through her blonde waves. "You know that Benton and I used to work together?"

Maggie thought back to their encounter at The Busy Bean. "I gathered something like that."

The reporter took a sip of tea. "Actually, it was me who brought Benton into the network." Stella stared into space, blinking, and Maggie had the sense that she was trying to suppress emotion. "I'm the one who pitched the idea to the head honcho. Underwater treasure hunting as a reality show. We already had *Geiger Gophers* and *Flea Market Finders*. Why not *Secrets of the Deep*? My title, by the way. I like it better than the one they changed it to." She snorted. "*Deep Sea Secrets* indeed."

"Wow. That was a lucky break for him."

"Wasn't it? When they say it's who you know, it's absolutely true." Stella traced a line on the tabletop with her finger. "They also say to keep your friends close and your enemies closer."

Maggie appreciated the background information, but her main concern was what Stella was going to do about Maggie's slipup. "So is Benton a friend or an enemy?" She tried to inject laughter into her tone to lighten things up.

"I don't know. Both, maybe? All I know is he promised to give me a series of exclusive interviews for my show. But now he isn't returning my calls. At all. He's freezing me out."

"And you want me to put in a word for you?" Maggie guessed that would be the price of Stella keeping quiet.

Stella shot her an amused glance. "I wasn't thinking that, but yes, that would be wonderful. I was actually hoping you'd agree to appear on my show."

"Do I have a choice?" *Doubt it.*

"You're an unusual woman, Maggie. I don't usually have to blackmail people into being on my show. It's very well regarded."

"I'm sure it is. I just don't have a strong desire to be on television." Maggie reached out to pat Snickers, who had come downstairs to join them. "I won't reveal any secrets on air, so please don't try to broadside me with anything."

"I don't do that." Stella sounded offended. "My show is on the up-and-up, not like tabloid reporting. That's one difference between my new employer and my old."

"Good to know. Addison Stringfellow doesn't share your scruples. He surprised me earlier today with something unflattering about Abigail Sedgwick." Maggie put a hand to her mouth. There she went again, speaking without thinking first.

"What did he say?" Stella's gaze sharpened.

Maggie waved a hand, trying to act as though it were something minor. "Oh, she apparently gave some artists lodging and a meal, and they turned out to be Confederate spies. Addison thinks she knew exactly who they were. I don't agree, of course."

Stella reared back. "I highly doubt she took in spies knowingly. Not here in Maine, the heart of Union country." She put a hand on Maggie's arm. "Listen, I'll make sure your side—Thomas and Abigail's side—is told. How's that?"

It was a nice offer, and even if Maggie happened to be wrong about the Sedgwicks, Stella would still have a good story. "Thanks, Stella. It's a deal."

Stella left shortly thereafter, and a disgruntled Maggie clumped back upstairs to her search, Snickers at her heels. To be on the safe side, she wouldn't answer her phone or the door for the rest of the day. She was too much of a blabbermouth. In addition, she didn't trust Stella or Benton's team—or any media professionals, for that matter. They would use whatever they could to their advantage. It was the nature of the business. It was up to her to ferret out the truth and make sure it was heard.

Assuming her quest for truth went the way she hoped. *What if I'm wrong, and both Thomas and Abigail were staunch rebels, working secretly against their government?* Maggie sighed. Then she'd have to suck it up and face the fact that every family had skeletons in its closet. Or as Daisy liked to say, every garden had its weeds.

This time she was able to retrieve the trunk from its tight spot without interruption, and she decided to take it to the office before looking through the contents. She verified that it contained papers before hauling it downstairs.

Snickers watched as she set the trunk on the desk. "Are you ready for the big reveal?" she asked him. His stare seemed to imply consent, so she opened the lid again, thankful it hadn't been locked.

Right on top was a brown leather journal, and when Maggie peered at the first page, she saw it was dated 1864. Her pulse leaped. Had this journal belonged to Abigail? There was no name written inside, but spidery brown handwriting detailed the weather, major expenditures, and events of note for each day.

She glanced through the entries, hoping to find some kind of proof one way or the other. An April entry read:

> *Mrs. Bennett delivered the new curtains for the manor library. Dark green damask velvet with gold satin lining.*

So the diary must have been Abigail's. Was the seamstress James Bennett's ancestor? She'd have to ask Deborah, his mother, who was a talented quilter.

Her cell phone rang and despite her resolution not to take calls, Maggie answered when she saw Ruth Harper was on the line.

"Hi, Maggie. I just wanted to remind you about the historical society meeting tonight." Ruth chuckled. "I know you've been busy with the treasure hunt and appearing on TV, but I was hoping you'd be able to join us."

Maggie glanced into the trunk, filled to the brim with layers of papers and letters. "How do you feel about helping me with a project? I've got Abigail Sedgwick's papers here and they need to be sorted."

Ruth's tone was emphatic. "Of course we'll help. Maybe we can find something related to the shipwreck."

"That's my hope too, Ruth."

After she hung up, Maggie gently placed the diary on top of the other papers. "You know what, Snickers? I'm going to give this a rest until tonight. Right now I'd better head over to the shop to help June before she disowns me."

. . . .

"Yum. These cookies are delicious." Maggie took another bite of the confection, which resembled a miniature cushion filled with raspberry jam. The historical society meetings always started with refreshments and coffee supplied by the members in rotation.

"Thanks," Deborah Bennett said. "I found the recipe in my grandmother's recipe box. They're old-fashioned, but tasty."

"My mother used to make them with dates," Ina said. "Or raisins."

Daisy entered the room, pulling a clear rain bonnet off her beehive hairstyle. "It's raining so hard the animals are starting to pair up." Peeling off her slicker, she glanced around. "Everyone made it, I see." In addition to Maggie, Ina, Ruth, and Deborah, the other members in attendance were June, Fran Vosburg, and Liz Young.

"We did, even though it is a miserable night out there," Ruth said. "After you grab something to eat, Daisy, why don't we get started? I thought we'd do our business and then help Maggie sort through the papers in Abigail Sedgwick's trunk."

The others hadn't heard about the trunk, and the news was met with gasps and exclamations of excitement.

"Another find from the famous second-floor storeroom?" Liz asked.

"That's right," Maggie said. "I found it today."

"I hope we can prove that professor is plumb wrong about Abigail and Thomas," Ina said. "I'd like to take him down a peg or two."

"His certainty about their support of the rebels annoys me too," Maggie said. "But I'm trying to keep an open mind."

The older woman scoffed. "You know what they say about some people? Their minds are like concrete, all mixed up and permanently set. Addison Stringfellow is one of those."

"Ladies, let's get to that later," Ruth said. "I have a few items to discuss."

Everyone settled down to participate in the discussion led by Ruth, which mostly concerned an upcoming fundraiser for the museum, housed in the Queen Anne house deeded to the society by the former resident. Like most old buildings, this one constantly needed repair. In addition, they were always seeking to expand their collection and host interesting exhibits, and that required funding too.

After they adjourned the business portion of the meeting, they cleaned up the refreshments and donned white gloves to help Maggie look through the papers. The thin cotton gloves were a precaution against soiling the ancient papers and perhaps damaging something of prime historical interest.

The piles of papers were lined up along the middle of the table, with each woman taking something and reading it. Maggie chose the journal, determined to find out if there was anything about the artist spies and the shipwreck written within.

There was silence for a few minutes, the only sounds the rustling of papers and the clearing of a throat or shifting in a seat. Maggie skipped ahead to the month of June, figuring that artists wouldn't be touring the coast much earlier than that due to weather. Halfway through July, she was rewarded. "Listen, everyone. I've found an entry about the spies."

Once Maggie had their attention, she read:

> The hot weather continues unabated. Well over eighty degrees today, and the leaves on the maples look limp for want of rain. A party of artists is painting on the shore nearby and when they inquired about a place to lodge, I offered them a meal and a night's board. It's lonely here. Thomas has been at sea for months.

"That doesn't sound like she knew they were spies," June said.

"I agree," Fran said. "Who bothers to lie in their diary? If she was afraid of someone reading it, she would probably leave the whole thing out."

"Well, most people don't lie in their diaries," Daisy said. "But I used to put fake stories in mine just to plague my sister."

Everyone laughed, then went back to reading. Not seeing anything further about the artists, Maggie leafed ahead to September 12, 1864, the day of the bank robbery.

> *First red leaves spotted today, which means winter will soon be upon us. Thomas will be home any day according to his last letter. In his honor, we've cleaned the manor and laid in a supply of his favorite foods.*

Sadness panged Maggie's heart. *Poor Abigail, preparing a homecoming for a man who never arrived.* That was the last entry in the diary.

Liz gave a gasp of excitement. "Oh my, you won't believe this."

"Don't keep us dangling, woman," Ina said. "What is it?"

"It's a nasty letter calling Thomas a traitor. Unsigned, of course."

"I have one too," Fran said, her cheeks pinking. She pressed her lips together. "It's vile."

"No wonder Abigail went into seclusion," Daisy said. "What came next, pitchforks and flaming torches?"

"So instead of receiving sympathy and support after the shipwreck, like any widow deserves, Abigail was hounded and maligned." The normally placid Liz was rigid with indignation. She slapped the table. "How dare they?"

"Maybe I'm lucky, since all I got was a skeleton sitting by my door," Maggie said.

June, Ina, and Daisy knew about the incident but the others exclaimed in shock.

"That's horrible," Fran said. "Downright mean."

"It was probably just a prank," Maggie said, warmed by her friends' support. Even though Thomas and Abigail had lived over a century ago, the ladies of the historical society still sympathized with the couple's plight. "Thanks for being on my side even though all the evidence seems to point the other way." She waved the diary.

"Don't show that to Stringfellow," Ina said. "He'll use it as proof somehow."

Ruth adjusted her glasses. "Unfortunately a lot of things are open to interpretation. We need to find something from either Thomas or Abigail that addresses the issue directly."

"Maybe the *Abigail's* figurehead will help," Maggie said. "Aunt Evelyn's journal implied that it held proof of Thomas's innocence."

"Something survived the shipwreck?" Daisy asked.

Maggie realized she hadn't told anyone but June about Evelyn's entry, and she quickly filled them in. "Addison e-mailed me a photo of the *Abigail,* so I'm going to enlarge it and see if I can discern any details of the figurehead. That might help us locate it."

"Maybe there's something about it in these papers," Ruth said. With that, they got back to work.

A short while later, Deborah called out, "I've got something here." Once she had everyone's attention, she continued, "You know how they said no one survived the shipwreck? Well, they were wrong."

She cleared her throat and read:

Dear Mrs. Sedgwick,

I'm writing this letter for my husband, Lemuel, one of the Abigail's sailors. He was fortunate to survive the wreck of the Abigail, but has since caught lung fever from his time

in the frigid waters. The doctor doesn't give much hope, and
I've called the preacher.

Deborah paused, clearing her throat again. "This is so sad."
She went on:

> Despite his discomfort, he insisted I write to you so your
> mind might be set at ease. He says your husband was a fine
> man, a man of honor and integrity, the best he ever worked
> for. He is innocent of any wrongdoing, as are all the crew of
> the Abigail. There is proof, he says, because he saw it in the
> captain's hand. He urges you to find it.
>
> Yours sincerely, Mary Jenkins.

Two things about the letter struck Maggie. One, proof
existed—or had existed—of Thomas's innocence. Two, Lemuel
Jenkins had the same last name as Clem, the doomsayer at the
docks. Could they be related?

Did Clem have the information she needed?

10

The next morning, Maggie saw that the rain had stopped, but the day was socked in and overcast. After breakfast, she dressed warmly and threw on a raincoat before making her way down to the docks. She was due to board the *Deep Six* in an hour, but she had another stop she wanted to make first.

The area of town past the working section of the docks was isolated, containing only a few shanties strung along the rocky shore near an old canning factory. Most had begun life as bait sheds and boathouses. Someday they would likely be torn down and have condos built in their place, but presently they housed some of Somerset Harbor's poorest citizens.

Maggie liked walking along the water in all weather, including fog. The dense bank of clouds reduced visibility to mere feet, wisps of vapor drifting in the air and touching her face with cool fingers. A buoy clanged out in the harbor, and over at the lighthouse, a foghorn blatted intermittently.

Clem Jenkins lived in the shack at the end, which had peeling red paint and a front porch cluttered with pot buoys, nets, clam rakes, and oars. Out in front of the house, a dinghy was drawn up on the shingle. Maggie remembered Daisy saying the old salt fished and dug clams for a living.

Sweet-scented woodsmoke poured out of the metal chimney, which she took to mean that someone was home. She climbed creaky, warped stairs and crossed the slanted porch to the front door. A dingy curtain over the window blocked her view of the interior.

Maggie rapped on the glass. No answer, so she knocked again. This time she was rewarded by the sound of shuffling footsteps.

The curtain twitched and then the door opened. Clem blinked watery eyes against the daylight, dim as it was. His chin and cheeks were covered with gray bristles, and his hair stood on end.

Maggie felt a rush of contrition. "Did I wake you? I'm sorry."

He grumbled an answer that apparently wasn't meant for her ears, then raised his voice enough so she could hear. "Was there anything in particular you wanted?"

She shifted from foot to foot. Apparently she wasn't going to get an invitation to enter, which, judging by the amount of belongings stuffed inside, she didn't regret.

"Last night at the historical society meeting we came across a letter from a Mrs. Lemuel Jenkins. Was she your ancestor?"

Clem scratched his chin and eyed her with suspicion. "Maybe. Why?"

"The letter said that her husband was on the *Abigail*. And—"

"Not that old scuttlebutt again!" Clem's hands curled into fists. "I won't have you interfering biddies raking up my family history." His gaunt face turned an alarming shade of red. "It took us a hundred years to live it down the first time."

"Clem." Maggie put up a staying hand. "Hold on. We're in the same boat. My family was tarred with the same brush."

He squinted one eye. "So? You ain't done too badly, living in that mansion."

She had to admit he was right. "I'm guessing you are related to Lemuel Jenkins. I found a letter from his wife written to Abigail Sedgwick after the *Abigail* sank. Did the shipwreck hurt your family?"

His mouth dropped open. "Did the shipwreck hurt my family?" His tone was scornful. "What do you think? My great-grandmother was left a widow with nothing, and for a couple of generations after, men in my family had trouble getting work. We were branded as traitors."

"So I'm guessing the salvage of the shipwreck brought all of this up again for you." Even though it was doubtful the treasure hunt would hurt Clem financially or in any other way, it was painful to have one's family history called into question, as she knew all too well.

His face softened slightly. "It's rough on you too, isn't it? They threw the most mud at Thomas Sedgwick. As captain, he took flack for allowing them rebels to take over his ship." He spit, aiming the glob a little too close to Maggie's shoes. "Of course they said he was in cahoots with them. I don't believe that for one second."

Maggie stepped back a pace, hoping he wouldn't spit again. "I'm in agreement with you, Clem. But tell me, why are you so certain the ship is jinxed? Because of your family history?"

A crafty look darted across his face. "Nope. I've seen some downright evil doings going on, I tell you."

"What do you mean?" Had Clem seen something suspicious regarding the television crew or the *Deep Six*?

He began to close the door. "That's all I've got to say on the subject." The door slammed shut.

Clem refused to answer the door again, so Maggie gave up and went back to the docks. Harry was there with the dinghy. "We're not going out today, are we?" she asked him, concerned about the low visibility across the water.

"No. It's way too foggy," was the lobsterman's expert opinion. "Benton said we'd film demos of the technical systems for filler on the show." Harry glanced out at the *Deep Six*, almost invisible as the pea soup deepened. "You probably don't even need to be there."

"I'm here, so I might as well go out." After visiting Clem, Maggie was eager to see if she could spot any sign of "evil doings" out on the boat.

"All right. Hop in then." Harry thrust out his hand for her to grab.

This time, climbing up the ladder to the deck wasn't such an ordeal, and Maggie was pleased with herself for being so adventurous. No one was out on deck, and the boat rose and fell in the chop, metal ringing as pieces of rigging collided.

Captain Gene was in the lounge, playing cards with several men Maggie recognized as belonging to the ship's crew. "Hey, Miss Maggie, what happens when the fog lifts in California?" Gene asked. Leaning back on his chair's rear legs, he winked up at her.

With a sigh, Maggie decided to slow her pace and humor him. "I don't know, what happens when the fog lifts in California?"

"UCLA." With one of his belly laughs, Gene thumped his chair down. "UCLA. Get it?"

Maggie fought the urge to roll her eyes. "I do." *Unfortunately.* She walked on, hurrying to join Harry, who was waiting at the door to the lower deck.

"I can't stand that guy," Harry said as he followed her down the stairs. "I can't believe Benton hired such a clown."

"I think it was Addison's recommendation, and they were stuck."

"I'd have to be desperate before I'd hire him. Even if he does know his way around a ship." At the door to the command center, Harry said, "I'm going to leave you here. I'll be up on the bridge looking at the weather if you need me."

Inside the command center, Benton was conferring with Chris and Nate, the show's production manager, about what he wanted filmed, while Kristen and Addison looked on. "I'm thinking we can take people through the steps of mapping the ocean floor and enhancing the photographs."

"We already got some of that the other day, with Maggie." Chris nodded a greeting to her and she waved.

"True." Benton leaned back against the desk, crossing his

arms. "But I've learned the hard way to get lots of B footage. Then if there's a dead spot, we'll have filler."

"Sounds good. Give me a minute and we'll roll." Chris fiddled with the settings on his camera.

"Go ahead and power up the sonar programs," Benton told Eric. He extended a hand to Maggie. "How are you?"

"Great, thanks." Maggie glanced around. "Rory off today?" she asked.

"He's under the weather, I'm afraid." Benton grimaced. "Bad clam or something."

"Sorry to hear that." Maggie put a hand to her belly in sympathy.

"We're all set, Benton." Eric swiveled in his chair to face them, then turned back to the monitors.

"Great, thanks." Benton gave Nate a thumbs-up. "Ready. Chris?"

Chris already had his eye to the viewfinder. "Ready."

Maggie sat back out of camera range, glad not to have to do anything but watch. They were about five minutes into Benton's demonstration when she smelled something strange. Hot, like burning plastic. She glanced around. Was something sitting on a burner somewhere, like a melting coffeepot?

The odor grew stronger. "Uh-oh." Eric pushed back his chair, interrupting Benton. "Something is on fire." The technician dashed to a closet door in the corner and wrenched it open, revealing an array of equipment crisscrossed with multiple wires. "Just as I thought. Electrical fire."

Benton was on his heels, neck craning. "Where's it coming from?"

"I'm not sure, but we need an extinguisher stat."

"Where are they?" Chris sent a wild glance around the room. "I don't see one in here."

"You're kidding. There's supposed to be one in the room." Benton snapped his fingers and pointed. "Go upstairs, quick, and find one."

Maggie was already at the door. She went into the corridor and up the steps, yelling, "Fire! Fire!"

Crewmen came running. The next little while was a confusion of shouting, pushing, spraying of extinguishers, and finally, relief when the fire was judged to be out. The crewmen went back to their stations, leaving Captain Gene and Harry to confer with Benton about the situation.

"You caught it early and that's good," Captain Gene said. "But I'm afraid you're going to have to get someone in here to check all the wiring and fix whatever shorted."

Benton groaned. "That means we're dead in the water. We can't go back out to the site without Spot's monitoring equipment." He collapsed into a chair. "The network's not going to be happy with this delay." Looking up at Harry, he asked, "Is there anyone local who can do the repairs?"

Harry shook his head. "Not that I know of. You'll have to call someone in Portland or Boston."

With a sigh, Benton pushed himself out of the chair. "I guess I'd better get on it." Catching Maggie's eye, he attempted a smile. "Another spoke in the wheel of progress, right? Want to join us at the hotel tonight for commiseration and dinner?"

"Sure, I'll be there." Maggie felt sorry for Benton, who appeared disheartened by the latest problem. The safety of the gold stash came to mind. The longer they waited to retrieve it, the greater the chance that someone else would scoop it up right out from under Benton's nose. Sure, they were sworn to secrecy, but news about treasure for the taking was bound to travel fast.

· · · · · · · · · · · · · · · · ·

The first thing Maggie saw when she entered Carriage House Antiques that afternoon was a carved wooden box standing on a table. She called, "June, where did this box come from? It's kind of nice."

June strolled out of the back room, carrying a coffee mug. "I thought you bought it."

"No, I didn't." Maggie reached out and tested the latch. It was unlocked.

June took a sip of coffee. "It was outside the door in a box addressed to you when I got here this morning."

"That's strange." Maggie flipped the lid open as the front door rattled and James walked in. The gust of air from outside disturbed the contents of the box, and dozens of tiny white feathers flew into the air, drifting all over the shop.

James reached up and caught one. "What . . . ?"

"I don't know," Maggie said. "I think it's another little 'gift.' What do you think it means?"

"I know people gave out white feathers during wartime. It was usually a symbol of cowardice," June said.

James set his lips in a grim line. "This is getting absurd."

"Is there anything else inside?" June asked.

After digging around gently to keep more feathers from fluttering out of the box, Maggie pulled out a small slip of paper. *A note.* The words scrawled there chilled her to her core. "What does it say, Maggie?" James reached out to take the paper Maggie offered him and read it:

You can't fly away from your past, TRAITOR.

"Who would do something like this?" he asked.

Maggie shook her head in disbelief. "Where's the cardboard box it came in, June? Did you keep it?"

"Sure did. I broke it down and put it with the others." They kept a stack of cardboard boxes on hand. "I'll go get it."

The box held only a printed label with Maggie's name and the shop address, with no return address or evidence of postage or shipping paid.

"This was dropped off here by someone," James said.

"Let's put it back in the box," Maggie said, "and I'll take it to the police station later. I want it out of here."

Using gloves just in case, Maggie put the box of feathers in the storeroom. She was getting a taste of what Abigail Sedgwick and Clem Jenkins's family had gone through and it wasn't fun.

Back in the main room, June was showing James a pair of Windsor chairs that needed glue, so Maggie went to the computer station. She still hadn't had a chance to enlarge the photograph of the *Abigail,* and there was no time like the present. She felt the need to do something in the wake of the unsettling surprise she'd received. Maggie downloaded the photograph from her e-mail and saved it to the computer, then opened a photo program. Fortunately Addison's photo was a high-enough resolution that she was able to enlarge the picture without it becoming fuzzy. She zoomed in on the front of the ship. The figurehead looked like a statue of a woman rather than a mermaid or other mythical creature. It actually resembled the portrait of Abigail, which was fitting since the ship was named for her.

"June, come here," Maggie called. "Tell me if you've seen this figurehead anywhere."

The shop manager soon peered over her shoulder. "Yes, I have. It's up in the attic. I thought it was a statue." She cracked up. "Evelyn and I used to string her with lights at Christmas."

After getting directions from June, James wrestled the wooden woman downstairs and into the main storeroom. "Whew. She's quite heavy." James wiped his brow with a tissue. He knocked on the carved wood. "That's mostly solid."

Since it had a flat base, the life-size piece stood on its own without support. Finely carved, the figurehead featured a chignon hairstyle, a flowing dress, and a tranquil expression. The woman's right hand rested on her heart. The wood had once been painted, but water, salt spray, and time had weathered the finish so that the bare wood showed through the remaining flecks of color.

"She's beautiful." Maggie circled the figurehead with the eerie sense that she was viewing a lifelike representation of the woman for whom her home had been built.

"I almost expect her to talk to us," June said. "If only Evelyn had told me what she meant by that entry."

"I wish she had too," Maggie said. "And it makes me wonder if the proof Mary Jenkins mentioned in the letter to Abigail had something to do with this figurehead. I can't understand how it would, though."

James hunkered down to examine the base of the piece. "I do see something odd. I think it was attached to the ship down here. When the ship broke apart, the figurehead would most likely have split away unevenly."

"But the base is level," Maggie said. "Otherwise it wouldn't stand upright."

"Right." James straightened with a nod. "Maybe Captain Sedgwick chopped the figurehead off the ship so it wouldn't go to the bottom. But how would he have known to do that?"

Maggie reached out and stroked the statue's smooth cheek. "What secrets are you hiding, Abigail?"

11

Before leaving with the chairs he planned to repair, James moved the figurehead to the back room. "I have an idea about what to do next," he said, pushing the statue back against the wall. "Let me make a call or two."

"Thanks for your help, James." Maggie really was grateful she could depend on him. He was always there for her—helpful, kind, and fun to be with. "Would you like to go out to dinner tonight?" she asked on impulse.

He cocked his head. "Maybe. Where are you taking me?" He grinned, letting her know he was teasing.

Maggie laughed. "The television crew is gathering for dinner at the Oceanview, and I thought you might like to join us."

"Sure. Sounds good—as long as Captain Gene isn't there." James shuddered.

"He better not be. Tell you what, if he is, we'll eat by ourselves."

"It's a deal. Pick you up at six?"

"Sure. But only if I can pay." Maggie shook her finger at him.

"If you insist." James gave a mock sigh.

James left shortly afterward, followed by a flurry of customers coming in. Maggie noticed that they often seemed to come in bunches, and it kept her and June busy. The last of that group was walking out the door when another customer entered—Meredith Lee, elegant in a fitted gray trench coat and matching boots. Maggie hadn't seen her for a few days and had wondered if she'd left town. Apparently she had not.

"Oh, how quaint," Meredith said. "I absolutely love rustic little shops like this."

Rustic? "Thanks," Maggie said. "We enjoy it. Is there anything in particular you're looking for, or did you just want to browse?"

Meredith paused to admire the Samuel Ranlet clock. "Well, I'd like to tuck that grandfather clock in my suitcase, but I don't think it would fit."

"We can ship," June said. "Anywhere in the continental United States."

"Good to know." Meredith wandered over to the jewelry case. While not a focus for Carriage House Antiques, a small selection of estate jewelry was often on hand. "Usually when I travel, I pick up a piece of jewelry as a memento."

"Let me know if you want to see anything." Maggie pulled out the black velvet cloth they used to display the pieces for close customer viewing and set it on the glass countertop.

"I like those earrings." Meredith pointed a painted fingernail at a pair of gold chandelier earrings set with pearls.

Maggie unlocked the back of the case and pulled them out. "You can try them on if you want." She brought over a small standing mirror for Meredith to use.

"I'll do that, thanks." Meredith pulled out the diamond stud earrings she was wearing and set them on the velvet.

"I thought maybe you had left Somerset Harbor," Maggie said. "I haven't seen you around." She was merely making chitchat, so she was surprised at Meredith's scowl.

"I'm not going anywhere until they finish that salvage operation." Meredith tossed her blonde hair over one shoulder, then picked up one of the dangling earrings.

"Oh, are you involved with the show?" Maggie remembered Chris and Kristen discussing how Meredith had behaved on camera.

"Heck no. Or should I say, not yet." Meredith hooked the piece of jewelry in her ear and bent forward to peer at her reflection. "No, I'm here to support my husband." Perhaps the divorce was off. *If so, good for Meredith and Benton.* Maggie hated to see couples split.

Meredith put on the second earring. "We've had our differences, all right." She gave a little laugh, as if aware she'd answered Maggie's thoughts. "Like most couples. But I'm so excited about being here for him with this project. It's one of his biggest finds so far." She smiled in gleeful satisfaction, squeezing her eyes shut and shaking her head so the earrings tinkled. "Imagine. All that gold, lying there for the taking."

June, dusting an intricately carved armoire nearby, raised a skeptical eyebrow. After Meredith paid and left, she said, "Nothing like the promise of riches to make a woman overlook a man's faults."

Maggie thought about June's words as James drove them down to the Oceanview that evening. As the wife of a college professor, she'd been comfortable but never rich. But had she ever craved more material wealth? She had to say no. She had valued the quality of her relationship with Richard far more than the size of the paycheck he brought home.

"There's something about gold that brings out the worst in people," she mused.

James nudged her playfully with his elbow. "Present company excluded, right?"

"Oh, did I say that out loud? Sorry. I was thinking about something."

"It's okay. I've been known to talk to myself a time or two," James said. "By the way, I got in touch with my art historian contact this afternoon."

Maggie was touched by his readiness to help her. "Already? That was fast."

"I know you're eager to solve the mystery of the figurehead."

He gave her a knowing look. "Anyway, we can have it x-rayed. Then if there is something inside—"

Maggie gave a yelp and put her hand on his arm. Then she pulled it back with a blush. She usually didn't touch James spontaneously. "Thank you! That's so exciting!"

"I think so too." James pulled the Mercedes around to the front of the hotel, and a valet stepped forward and opened Maggie's door. As Maggie got out, she glanced up at the hotel's elegant, old-fashioned façade. Lights shone in the downstairs public rooms and in many of the guest rooms in the three-story structure. The high season was obviously extending past Labor Day this year. Or was it the salvaging of the *Abigail* that had brought so many to town?

The lobby bustled with guests, some heading into the lounge for drinks and others checking in or visiting with friends. Maggie checked with the hostess and learned that Benton's party was on the glassed-in porch, a private room off the dining area.

Benton stood to greet them as they entered. "Maggie, I'm glad you found us. I had to seclude us in here so we wouldn't be hounded by people with inquiring minds." In addition to Benton, Rory, Addison, Meredith, Daisy, and Harry were seated at the long table. Fortunately the captain was nowhere to be seen, but without his obnoxious manner, the mood was definitely subdued.

Maggie slid into a seat between Rory and Addison. James sat across from her, between Daisy and Meredith. Meredith was wearing the new earrings she'd purchased at the shop, Maggie noticed, along with a pink shantung silk sheath. She looked stunning, as did Daisy, dressed in a red suit that set off her dark hair. Maggie was glad she had worn a sleek navy pantsuit.

"Are you feeling better?" Maggie asked Rory. She unfolded her cloth napkin and settled it on her lap.

Rory grimaced as he rubbed his midsection. "I've been better, mate. But I'm sticking to light food, so I'm managing."

"You didn't get sick eating here, I hope." Daisy frowned. She took it to heart when the reputations of the eateries in Somerset Harbor were in question, since she owned one too.

"No. I made the mistake of eating at one of those greasy little shacks along Route 1." Rory picked up the menu and studied it. "The food is stellar here."

Maggie thought so too, and she selected one of the specials, a baked seafood pasta dish with a large green salad on the side. Lots of hot bubbling cheese and savory morsels of freshly caught shrimp and scallops. James ordered the same.

After they were served salad and bread, James asked, "How's the salvage operation going?"

Rory scoffed. "Terrible. A few minutes ago we got the news that the electronics won't be fixed for close to a week."

Benton poured himself another glass of wine and took a sip. "All these delays are eating up our working capital. Our investors aren't happy."

James sent Maggie a look of alarm. "Sorry to bring up a painful topic. I had no idea."

"The worst part is that we've got other treasure hunters on the trail already." Addison sniffed in demonstration. "And the media."

Meredith gasped, one hand flying to her necklace. "Is someone else going to get to the gold first?"

"Assuming there is gold to be found down there," Benton said, casting a pointed look at Addison. "There's always a danger of that. Rumor of treasure is like blood in the water in shark territory."

Was this all true or was it more drama staged for the show? Maggie didn't see a camera anywhere, but that didn't mean much. Maybe they hid one in the ceiling or someone was covertly filming with their phone. "Are you serious?" she asked. "Is the treasure hunt really in jeopardy, or is this conversation just part of the show?"

Rory barked a laugh. "You're catching on quick, my dear. But this isn't scripted dialogue. We're basically dead in the water at the moment."

Maggie's mind whirled so much through the rest of the meal that she barely tasted her food or heard the conversation around her.

"Well, that was a gloomy dinner," she said to James later that evening, after the two of them had enjoyed coffee in the lounge and headed out for a stroll. "And Benton was drinking way too much." They walked along the shore path that fronted the hotel and led to the docks, the gravel crunching under their shoes. The way was lit with charming standing lights that resembled gas lanterns. "I'm sorry to put you through that."

"No problem. The meal was tasty." James smiled down at Maggie. "And the company was great. Some of it, anyway."

Maggie felt her cheeks flush. "I'm glad you think so." They paused by one of the benches situated with a stunning view of the harbor. Lights twinkled along the shore, strung like jewels among the dark hills and on the *Deep Six*'s antennas out in the bay. "This is pretty." She took a deep breath of salty air, enjoying the light breeze against her face.

"It is. I like walking at night." James fell silent, and they continued along to the docks in quiet contentment. "Want to go down and look at the boats?"

Although the season was nearing its end, lobster and fishing boats as well as a few pleasure craft remained in their slips. A series of floating docks led to them, rising and falling with the tide. At the end of one wide dock stood a small gazebo with tiny lights trimming its roof. It was a prime spot for tourist photographs and courting couples.

Maggie's heart skipped a beat as James steered her in that direction. Since it was night, they certainly weren't there for pictures. She glanced up at his chiseled profile with a thrill of excitement. What was James thinking?

They reached the end of the dock and stepped into the gazebo. Still moving in one accord, they walked to the ocean side. "One of my favorite spots in town," James said. "I used to come here as a teenager all the time."

Maggie imagined a much younger James, tall and gangly but showing signs of the handsome man he would become. Had he brought a girlfriend?

Before she could ask—in a teasing way, of course—James gave a cry of alarm. "Look! Down there. See it?"

Maggie's gaze followed his pointing finger to the water, about three feet below. In the dim glow from a nearby light, she saw a man's body floating, the incoming tide bumping him in a gentle rhythm against the pylons.

He wasn't moving.

12

Maggie screamed. "Oh no! Do you think he's still alive? We need to help him!" She scanned the area, trying to figure out how to get down to where the man now rested against the underside of the dock. Could she climb over the gazebo railing?

James fumbled for his cell phone, tucked in his jacket pocket. "Call for an ambulance. And the police."

Maggie took the phone and dialed 911 with trembling fingers. James was stripping off his suit coat. "What are you doing?"

"I'm going to see if I can save him." James threw the jacket onto a bench and bent to slip off his shoes and socks. "You wait here, okay?"

While Maggie explained the situation to the dispatcher, her voice cracking with fear and horror, James climbed over the railing to the wide ledge below. As she hung up, she heard a splash. She ran to the railing. His head bobbed in the water nearby.

"James!" she called.

"I'm going to pull him in." James swam toward the underside of the wharf, where the tide had pushed the drowned man. "I can't sit here and wait."

Maggie shuddered, hugging herself. If only they had come down here earlier. Maybe they could have prevented this tragedy.

Within a minute or two, James emerged from under the wharf and began swimming toward shore, pulling the man by his coat. The strobing lights of a Somerset Harbor police cruiser, an ambulance, and a fire truck lit up the night sky as they raced into the parking lot and toward the docks.

"James is in the water!" Maggie yelled to Robert Linton as he jumped out of his cruiser. Robert shouted orders at the others and they swarmed down to the shore. An officer carrying a couple of standing lights set them in place. Two men wearing diving gear entered the water with a splash. One took charge of the immobile man while the other helped James out of the water.

Maggie ran along the dock. "James. Are you all right?"

James nodded, teeth chattering. "I have a bag of gym clothes in my car. Can you get them? My keys are in my jacket." An EMT draped a blanket around his shoulders and led him to the ambulance.

Officers and medical personnel surrounded the other man, and with a prayer for his life, Maggie sped on foot to the parking lot, where James had left the car. She quickly retrieved his duffel bag and ran back to the docks. Inside the ambulance, James toweled off and changed.

When he emerged, dressed in sweatpants, a T-shirt, and sneakers, Maggie rushed to his side, handing him his jacket. "Are you really okay?"

James nodded. "A little cold, but I'm fine." He drew her aside and lowered his voice. "Maggie, that was Benton Lee in the water."

Shock hollowed Maggie's belly. "Benton? Are you sure? But we just saw him at dinner."

"He was . . . ah . . . feeling no pain after all those drinks. He must have fallen off the dock into the water." James shook his head. "Tragic."

Robert Linton approached. "James. Thanks for your help out there."

"How is he?" James nodded toward the docks, where medical personnel still surrounded the prone figure of the television personality.

The officer shook his head. Without Robert saying a word, Maggie knew Benton was gone. Her knees gave out under her and only James's strong arm kept her from falling.

"I'm sorry to do this," Robert said, "but I need you both to hang around a few more minutes."

"We can do that," James said. "We'll wait over there." He pointed to a bench near a lamppost a short distance away.

"I appreciate it," Robert said. With a nod, he strode off, intent on his task.

In a daze, Maggie tottered along the dock, barely aware of her feet striking the boards. Benton Lee was dead. She couldn't believe it, couldn't accept it. She stumbled over something in her way, something she'd thought was a shadow.

"Careful." James reached out and grabbed her by the elbow.

"What was that?" Maggie bent to look. A navy blue wool peacoat lay on the dock. Many fishermen wore them, since the dense weave repelled water and wind.

She scooped it up and carried it to the bench, deciding it was too nice to leave out in the weather. Then she felt foolish. What did a coat matter when a man was dead? Her teeth began to chatter.

James took off his jacket and tucked it around her shoulders. "Hang on, Maggie. We can't have you going into shock."

"Don't you need this? You're the one who was wet." He shook his head and she huddled into his coat, grateful for the extra warmth.

Another couple came along the shore path, walking close and laughing. As they passed under a light, Maggie gasped. *Meredith and Rory.* She tapped James on the knee. "James, we need to stop them."

James stiffened when he saw the couple. They paused on the path, noticing the activity around the docks, and appeared poised to go down and find out what was going on. They weren't the only ones; a few onlookers had wandered into the parking lot and onto the docks as close as they dared. Somerset Harbor's gossip network was probably already humming.

"I'll go intercept them," James said. "Will you be all right?"

"Of course." Maggie clutched his jacket closer and watched as James approached Meredith and Rory. She couldn't hear more than a murmur of words, but she didn't need dialogue to interpret Meredith's cry of alarm as she launched herself into Rory's arms. He staggered back slightly, then recovered, patting her on the back as he asked James questions.

Observing the couple objectively this way, she did notice something discomfiting. Judging by their body language, the duo appeared unusually close. *More than friends?* Maggie remembered the conversation she had interrupted at the manor. *I'll take care of it,* Rory had said to Meredith. Had he meant her husband? Or rather, her soon-to-be-ex-husband?

But surely Benton's death was an accident. It had to be.

James guided a sobbing Meredith and a gray-faced Rory toward her. A couple of times Meredith tried to break away from Rory's encircling arm and dash down to the dock where Benton lay, and he had to forcibly restrain her. Maggie was overcome with sympathy at the heart-wrenching sight, which was stirring up unwelcome memories of her own loss. She, too, had experienced that horrified bewilderment.

With a masterful effort, she stuffed those emotions back in their box and locked them away, focusing instead on the situation at hand. Chief Rick Cole arrived right before a Volvo station wagon pulled in, and a man carrying a medical bag hurried down to the spot.

The coroner, Maggie guessed. She hoped his pronouncement would be fast and Robert Linton would be able to release them soon.

Rory and Meredith sat on a bench nearby, and James came back to join her. "I told them that Robert might want to talk to them, to find out when they last saw Benton," James said in a low voice. "Not my favorite moment, informing them about his death."

"You couldn't let them walk down there and find out that way," Maggie said. "That would have been cruel."

The coroner spent a few minutes examining the body, then rose to his feet, shaking his head. He conferred with Robert and the chief as the medical personnel closed up the body bag and lifted it onto the gurney. Huddled in the shelter of Rory's arm, Meredith kept her gaze averted, but the Australian watched the proceedings with grim determination.

As the gurney trundled up to the ambulance, Robert Linton and Chief Cole began to walk toward them. Other officers began to search the area, scanning the docks, decks of boats, and the parking lot.

"I'd better go tell them Benton's widow is here," James said, leaving the bench once again. After a brief conversation, James and the chief went to talk to Rory and Meredith while Robert came over to Maggie.

"Maggie, take me through the evening." While he took notes, she told him about the dinner, the walk afterward, and how she and James had come across the body. Out of the corner of her eye, she saw the drama unfolding a distance away as Chief Cole spoke to the others.

"So you didn't see Benton at all after dinner? At the hotel or along the path?"

Maggie shook her head. "No. We didn't see anyone." It struck her that he was asking an awful lot of questions for an accidental drowning. "Do you think Benton was murdered?"

Robert tightened his lips, glancing over at the chief. "You're going to hear this sooner or later anyway, so I suppose it's all right to tell you. Benton had some, ah, very suspicious marks on him."

"Like what?" Maggie imagined a knife or bullet wound.

"He was hit on the head." Robert rubbed the side of his head as if in sympathy. "And he had a black eye forming." He paused. "And we found something in his hand that clinches it."

"What was that?" Absently, Maggie picked up the peacoat and smoothed it over her lap.

Noticing what she was doing, Robert made a choking sound. "Where did you get that coat?"

"I found it on the docks, near the lobster boats." She reached into one of the side pockets and fished around. The only thing in there was a small card. She held it up to the light, squinting. "It's a dentist appointment card for Harry Carter. This coat must belong to him."

Robert held out his hand for the coat. Puzzled, Maggie handed it to him. He felt down the front, checking the buttons. Then he gave a piercing whistle, bringing another police officer running. "Take this into evidence."

13

"I don't understand," Maggie said. "Why is Harry's coat evidence?"

Looking uncomfortable, Robert adjusted his hat more firmly on his head and stood. "I'd better not go into it." He quickly turned and walked away to meet the chief, now headed their way.

"Maggie! What's going on?"

Maggie turned to see Captain Gene Percival. "Something terrible has happened. Benton Lee drowned." As she said the bald statement of fact, she felt tears thicken her throat. Her nose began to run, and she fumbled in her handbag for a tissue.

Gene collapsed on the bench beside her. "You're kiddin'." Then he gave a rueful chuckle. "Of course you're not. The police are crawlin' all over these docks." He was silent, his beady eyes darting around the scene. "I think I know who did it."

Maggie reared back. "Who? You saw something? You should tell the police."

"Tell us what, Maggie?" Robert was back, Chief Cole in tow. James was still taking to Meredith and Rory.

"Robert, Chief Cole, this is Gene Percival, captain of the *Deep Six*. He said he knows who killed Benton."

Chief Cole gave Gene the once-over. "Do tell, Captain. Time is of the essence."

Gene squirmed back and forth on the bench as though getting comfortable. He raised one thick finger, wagging it. "I didn't actually see Benton go in the water. But I did see him fightin' with someone. That lobsterman, Harry Carter."

A lance of shock pierced Maggie. Harry had been fighting with Benton?

Robert sent a pointed glance at the chief, who shook his head and sighed. "You'd better go pick him up, Robert. Bring him in for questioning."

Maggie jumped to her feet in protest. "You *can't* be serious. Harry wouldn't hurt a fly. Come on, Robert, you've known him all your life."

"I'm sorry, Maggie. We have to put our personal feelings aside in a case like this." Robert's expression was sad. "We have to go by the evidence." His gaze dropped to Gene, who was avidly listening. "And by eyewitness testimony."

. . . .

"James, I can't believe it," Maggie fumed as James drove her home a short while later. "They actually think Harry killed Benton."

Her cell phone dinged with a text from June. *Emergency society meeting at the Carters'. Can you come?*

She typed back, *YES. Be right there.*

"I'm as stunned as you are," James said. "But remember that all the evidence isn't in yet. Just because Harry had words with Benton doesn't mean he pushed him into the water."

"Hit him on the head and pushed him in, you mean," Maggie said. "They said Benton had marks on his body. And he was holding something in his hand. Something tied to Harry, I'm guessing."

James pulled into the manor's driveway and rolled to a stop. "Would you like me to come in? I'm not being forward, but I thought you might want some company. It's going to take me a while to digest it all, that's for sure."

"Thanks, James. That's a nice offer." Maggie waved her phone, then dropped it back into her purse. "But I'm going over to the Carters' with the girls."

"That sounds like a good idea. Daisy must be beside herself."

James patted Maggie on the shoulder. "Keep me posted, okay? I don't care if it's the middle of the night, I want to know if anything happens." The thought that Harry might be arrested and charged with murder lay unspoken between them.

On an impulse, Maggie leaned over and gave James a quick hug. "You're a good man, James Bennett. I'll keep you posted, promise."

After James pulled away, Maggie hopped into her car and zoomed over to the Carter residence. Their cozy Cape Cod, built by a Carter ancestor generations ago, was located on one of the residential streets overlooking the harbor. The short driveway was full of cars, so Maggie parked on the street in front.

June greeted her at the door. "Glad you could come. Harry's down at the station. He didn't want Daisy to go with him, so they questioned her here and then took him in. It's a good thing we're here. She's in a bad way."

Maggie stepped into the small foyer. As she took off her jacket and hung it on the hall tree, she saw the other society members gathered in the living room, where a fire roared in the huge brick fireplace. Tea, coffee, and cookies were set out on a coffee table.

"We thought this would take the chill off," Ina said, giving a log a poke.

"It's nice." Maggie found a seat on a plump ottoman near the armchair where Daisy sat. "How you holding up?" she asked her friend.

With a sniffle, Daisy shook her head. "I'll be better when Harry's back home." It was the first time Maggie had seen the Southern beauty without makeup, and she looked uncharacteristically wan. Even her usually bouncy hair was limp. "I can't imagine what Meredith is going through." She dabbed at her eyes.

"You are a good soul, worrying about someone else right now," Liz Young said. She perched on the long sofa between Fran and Ruth.

"Well, we were friends once." Daisy gave another sniff. "I forgave her years ago for stealing Benton out from under my nose."

"I heard it was you who found him," Ina said to Maggie. "That must have been awful."

Maggie shuddered. "James was with me. It was awful, though." Would she ever get the image out of her mind? She was almost afraid to go to sleep in case she dreamed about it.

Ruth adjusted her glasses. "Maggie, we're not being ghoulish here, but in the interests of helping Harry, we'd like to hear exactly what happened." She picked up a pad of paper and held a pen poised, as if taking minutes at a meeting.

Maggie explained how she and James had walked out to the gazebo and spotted Benton in the water. "The odd thing is, we didn't see a single soul along the shore path or down by the docks." She gulped, feeling responsible for Harry's trouble. "But I did find Harry's coat on the dock next to his boat. For some reason the police think it's evidence."

"His peacoat?" Daisy's mouth dropped open. "Someone stole it from the hotel."

"Aha!" Ina made a triumphant fist. "I knew we could clear him."

"If they'll believe us," Daisy said. "It sounds awfully convenient to say that someone else was wearing it."

"What happened after James and I left the dining room?" Maggie asked. "Take us through the rest of the night."

Daisy pushed back in the soft chair, her eyes on the crackling fire. "Let me see. After you two left, Addison, Rory, and Meredith also excused themselves. Harry and I stayed for dessert and coffee. I expected Benton to leave, but he just sat there." Her brows knit together in a frown. "I hate to speak ill of the dead, but Benton was drinking an awful lot. On top of the wine, he had several whiskeys."

"The truth is important no matter how ugly," Liz said.

"That's right." Fran nodded. "His drinking may have a bearing on the case."

Daisy snorted. "It had a bearing on his fight with Harry, that's for sure. After the second whiskey, Benton started being obnoxious, bragging and boasting about all he'd done, the people he knew in Hollywood, all that." She pursed her lips. "We could handle that but when he started needling Harry about being a small-town bumpkin, Harry got a little steamed. And then Benton implied I could have done better."

"That's not true." Ina's cottony hair practically stood on end with indignation. "There's no finer man on earth than Harry Carter."

"Thanks, Ina." Daisy gave her husband's champion a weak smile. "But that's not all. Benton started saying that he could have done better himself and he wished he had married me instead of the—and I quote—'gold digger.'"

"That must have gone over like a lead balloon," Ruth said, looking up from her writing.

"Exactly. Benton got up and wandered out the back exit, toward the shore. I thought that was the end of it, but Harry wanted to tell him off." Daisy's lips twisted in grimace. "I told him not to, but you know how stubborn he is." She shook her head. "A few minutes later he was back, sporting a black eye. And feeling like a fool."

"Harry had a black eye? Robert said Benton had one too," Maggie said.

"He gave as good as he got, huh?" Ina made fighting gestures with her tiny fists. "Good for him."

"Harry's not denying they had a fight," Daisy said, "but he didn't push Benton into the water. He was fine when Harry left him. Drunk and angry, but alive."

"Do you know what time that was, Daisy?" Ruth asked.

"Hmm. About nine thirty, maybe?"

"So someone killed him between nine thirty and ten thirty," Maggie said. "That's about when we found him." She remembered hearing the town clock strike ten while they were walking on the path.

"Let's make a list of suspects." Ina's eyes brightened with determination as she ticked them off. "We've got the estranged wife. The cohost. The professor. The captain or a crew member. The television crew, although I like those young 'uns . . ."

"Ina, slow down," Liz said with a laugh. "That's way too many people already."

"It might have been random," Fran said. "Was he robbed?"

"Possibly," Maggie said. "That would be simple." Although muggings were a very rare event in Somerset Harbor.

"We need to find out if they took Benton's wallet," Daisy said.

"I agree." Ruth made a note of that. "Let's talk about the others. Why would they kill Benton? Most of them seemed to be benefiting from his being around."

Ina put her hands on her hips. "Rory was ticked off that Benton was the main host. I read that in *Entertainment Inquirer*."

"That might not be the most reliable source," June said gently.

Ina's retort was tart. "Sure it is. Where there's smoke there's fire, I always say." Maggie smiled, as Ina had indeed said that very thing before the dinner party at Sedgwick Manor.

"We'll put it down as a theory." Ruth glanced around the room. "Any others?"

Daisy made a groan, a sick look on her face. She held up a hand. "Sorry. I just realized that it might have been Meredith who killed him, bless her heart." She blinked back tears. "But to say that out loud, even to think it, feels like a betrayal."

"We hear you," Liz said gently. "But we have to consider everyone with a possible motive. The police seem to have fastened on Harry. We're not going to let him get railroaded."

"Heck no." Ina stomped a foot. "Over my dead body."

"I might have something, though it seems like a long shot," Maggie said. "Remember Stella Marquez, the reporter from *Seacoast Today*? She claimed she helped Benton get the show when she worked for the network. Maybe there was bad blood there."

"We're looking at personal motives," June said. "But don't forget one huge financial motive: the possibility of gold on the *Abigail*."

As they sat in silence digesting this, a car pulled up in front of the house and a door slammed.

Ina peered outside. "Here comes Harry now."

Daisy hurried to greet her husband, everyone else staying in the living room to give them privacy for a few minutes.

Harry's brows rose when he entered the room. "Wow. I didn't expect to see all of you here." He slung an arm around Daisy's shoulders. "Thanks for supporting my wife."

"It's the least we could do for our good friends," Ruth said. "Besides, we know you're innocent." The others chimed in with agreement.

Harry rubbed his chin. "I appreciate that. They didn't formally charge me, which is a good thing, but I'm not off the hook yet."

"Was it a robbery, maybe?" Fran straightened, a hopeful look on her face.

"I asked the police that but they said nothing was missing. Benton still had his expensive watch and his wallet on him."

"So why do they think it was you?" Ruth asked. "Because of the argument?"

Harry pointed to his eye, which was indeed turning black and blue. "That's a nice way to put it, Ruth. We were going at it like two kids who don't know any better." He pressed his lips together. "Unfortunately they found something else that points the finger directly at me. Benton was holding a button from my coat. The one that was stolen."

All the pieces came together for Maggie, why the coat was abandoned and why Robert had taken it into evidence. "The person who took your coat must be the killer. We need to find out who that is."

The impromptu meeting broke up soon after, with assurances that they would solve the crime and, according to Ina, "show the police a thing or two." Totally exhausted after the long and draining day, Maggie drove slowly through the quiet streets. Her bed and cuddly cat beckoned. Maybe she could even sleep in for a change, since she didn't have any obligations the next day except the shop.

As she pulled the car into the driveway, her mind wandered to the TV show. Would it go on without Benton? To her surprise, she was disappointed at the idea that it might be cancelled. It had actually been fun. But at least she still had the mystery of Abigail and Thomas to dig into.

Thinking about the couple who had built the manor reminded Maggie that she was still carting Abigail's papers around in her car. Before she went inside, she opened the back door to retrieve the trunk of papers from the rear passenger seat.

It was gone.

14

Maggie searched the backseat again, coming up empty-handed. Hadn't she left the papers there? Maybe they were in the trunk of the car. She went around and checked there, but to no avail.

Someone stole Abigail's papers! With a rush of frustration, she stamped her foot. Who would want those papers? They weren't valuable, except to her.

Maggie shut the trunk and locked the car, thinking ruefully of barn doors and runaway horses as she went inside. No point in reporting the theft tonight. Robert Linton had more important things on his mind.

The missing papers capped off an already disturbed night. Worrying about Harry's situation and Benton's death, Maggie barely got a wink of sleep. As if in response to her distress, Snickers was also restless. He kept moving from spot to spot, at one point even trying to sleep on her head.

In a deep sleep at last, she was awakened by the phone ringing. After scrabbling around on the nightstand, she located it. "Hello?"

"Maggie. You've got to come down to the Bean right now." *Ina. She must be using someone else's phone since she doesn't own a cell.*

Maggie yawned. "What's going on? Ina, I'm not even dressed."

In response, Ina held the phone out so Maggie heard the sound of voices and clamor. "It's a media frenzy down here. You should see it."

"Because of Benton's death?"

"You got it. Hold on." She heard muffled sounds, then Ina said, "Yes, I knew him, quite well in fact. I was a PA on the shoot one day." She came back. "Gotta go. They want to interview me."

Maggie stared at the dead phone in bemusement. Ina was getting her fifteen minutes of fame, it appeared. She supposed she'd better go down and see if there were any updates on the case.

After showering and dressing in record time, Maggie headed on foot down the hill to the café. She'd thought about driving, but if it was as hectic as Ina said, then she wouldn't be able to find a parking space. As she drew closer, the mob scene on the docks confirmed her decision. There were even more people than the day Benton had announced the salvage operation. She saw half a dozen TV trucks, and she thought she spotted a reporter from a famous morning show standing with a microphone in hand.

"Treasure-hunting entrepreneur and television personality Benton Lee drowned last night in what police believe are suspicious circumstances . . . ," Maggie heard as she pushed past. So they hadn't officially ruled the death a murder. That was good news for Harry.

Ina darted through the crowd, wearing her PA cap, Maggie noticed with amusement. "Maggie! You're just in time. Rory is going to make an announcement to the press about the show."

Maggie saw that a podium had been set up near The Busy Bean, a setting all too reminiscent of Benton's optimistic and exciting announcement not so long ago. The Aussie strode up and took his place, holding both sides of the podium with his hands as if to steady himself.

He began by ducking his head as though in a moment of silence, a gesture that effectively silenced the crowd. He lifted his head. "Good day, ladies and gentlemen of the press, residents of Somerset Harbor. It's with great sorrow that I speak to you today." He paused, blinking back unshed tears. "Our good mate—our friend, Benton Lee, met with a tragic accident last night."

"An accident?" someone yelled from the crowd. "We heard it was murder!"

Rory held up a hand. "Hold on. There hasn't been an official ruling by the coroner yet."

There were a few more shouts and protests—including one from Stella Marquez, Maggie noticed—but the crowd soon piped down to listen.

"I'm sure you're wondering what's going to happen to our salvage operation. We were just getting under way and finding some encouraging results."

An understatement, Maggie knew.

People whistled, clapped, and cheered. "Did you find the gold yet?" someone shouted.

"I'm not at liberty to say anything more. But I assure you that I will as soon as possible." He nodded. "The network has decided that the show must go on."

"More like the investors decided," Ina said behind her hand.

"We will be continuing operations at the site of the *Abigail*. And I will be stepping into Benton's shoes. Not an easy feat, but one that I accept with the hope I can live up to his vision for our work and the show."

"Liar, liar, pants on fire," Ina said. Her voice wasn't quite low enough and a couple of people nearby turned to stare. "Let's go inside. I can see this confab is going to go on for a while, and I've heard all I need to."

The older woman led the way, and they sidled through the crowd to The Busy Bean's front door. Behind them, Rory continued to field questions from the voracious media. Sunken treasure and the death of a star. Interesting separately, but together they were a potent combination, especially if Benton's death was ruled to be a murder.

Inside, Daisy was running to and fro with the coffeepot. She was doing her best to be her usual bubbly, extroverted self, but there was a shadow of anxiety in her eyes. "Your table will be open in a minute if you hang on," she said as she buzzed past.

Maggie and Ina waited along the wall until the patrons occupying Maggie's favorite window table stood to leave, lingering as they put on jackets and fussed with their wallets. As soon as decently possible, Maggie and Ina snagged the seats, not caring if the dishes weren't cleared yet.

"I'll take care of these," Ina said, stacking plates and cups.

"And I'll help." Maggie picked up silverware and napkins, brushing crumbs off the table with her hands. Everything went into a nearby bus pan.

Daisy bustled up with two mugs and a coffeepot, clanking the cups down on the table. "What will it be?"

"I'll take one of Jack's egg sandwiches," Maggie said.

Ina nodded. "Make that two."

Maggie offered Daisy a supportive smile and asked, "How's Harry doing today?"

Daisy tilted her head toward the harbor. "He's out pulling traps. We're trying to keep things normal." She choked back a sob, blinking. "As if we can. Especially with that zoo right outside the front door."

The front door jingled and a half dozen more people surged inside, several wearing press badges.

"Well, at least you can make some money off 'em," Ina said.

"That's true. It will help us pay for bail." Daisy whirled away, pausing at other tables to pour refills.

"I've never seen Daisy like this." Frowning, Ina picked up her mug and held it in both hands. "She's usually so optimistic."

Maggie reflected on this. "You're right. But sometimes life deals a blow that you can't bounce back from immediately." She knew that firsthand.

"It only makes me more determined to get to the bottom of this mess," Ina said. "There's no way that Harry is guilty."

"Of course not. I'm hoping the coroner's report will prove that it was an accident."

"I doubt it." Ina tapped her chest. "I have a feeling it was murder." Glancing toward the door, her brows rose. "Don't look now, but we're being graced by the grieving widow."

Naturally Maggie turned to look and saw Meredith, all in black, slipping through the crowd that had gathered at the counter. Daisy set the pot of coffee down and hurried to greet her old friend. They embraced, then Daisy led her toward Maggie's table.

"Can Meredith sit with you?" Daisy asked. She snagged an empty chair from another table and set it at theirs.

Ina shifted over a little with a mumble.

"Of course," Maggie said. "Please sit down, Meredith."

Daisy pointed a finger at her friend. "Coffee? Egg sandwich?"

Meredith shook her head. "No thanks. I can't eat a thing. But yes to the coffee."

Daisy came right back with Meredith's coffee, followed by a waitress who deposited the sizzling, savory egg sandwiches in front of Maggie and Ina. The trio sat in silence for few minutes, focused on the view of the harbor outside the wide window. The day was bright and windy, and boats buzzed back and forth, bouncing in the chop.

Maggie wanted to extend sympathy to Meredith but was reluctant to probe the wound. She remembered being comforted by friends who merely sat quietly with her after Richard's death, so that's what she did. Fortunately, Ina followed her lead, seeming to take great interest in the antics of seagulls perched on dock pilings.

"Y'all are so sweet." Meredith pulled a pack of tissues out of her designer purse and dabbed her eyes. "Thanks for not barraging me with questions or sympathy."

"I'm sure you're getting enough of that already." Ina reached out and patted Meredith's arm. "The press out there is like a swarm of bees after honey."

"I simply can't believe it." Meredith ducked her blonde head. "He's really gone. Leaving me with nothing but regrets."

"Nothing?" Ina's brows knit together, but before she could say more, Maggie shook her head slightly.

"I hear you, Meredith," Maggie said. "I think it's human nature to question ourselves, to feel we could have done better, loved someone more." She and Richard had had an excellent marriage, but that didn't mean she didn't regret their rare arguments or the times she'd been self-absorbed rather than focused on her husband.

Meredith nodded. "Exactly." She picked up her mug in shaking hands and sipped.

Ina lurched back in her chair, her gaze fixed on the front door. "Uh-oh. Here comes trouble."

Maggie turned to see Stella Marquez bearing down on them. The reporter waved a hand. "Meredith! Meredith Lee." The other customers turned to stare.

Meredith spun in her seat. "Oh no. Here we go." She set down the mug and gathered her purse, clearly ready to flee.

Stella picked up her pace. Reaching the table, she said, "Meredith, I'm so sorry for your loss. Benton was a good friend of mine."

The tactic worked and Meredith relaxed. "Thanks, Stella. I know Benton valued your professional relationship. He always talked about how you got him the show."

"Did he?" Stella grimaced. "He often spoke of you too." She paused. "Isn't it true you signed a prenuptial agreement?"

Meredith blinked, obviously caught off guard by the question.

Stella continued as if she hadn't noticed Meredith's lack of response. "Good thing the divorce hadn't gone through yet." Her eyes narrowed as she waited for the effect of her words to fully sink in.

Red spots flamed in Meredith's cheeks. With a violent gesture she pushed back from the table and stood, forcing the reporter to step aside. "How dare you? Our marriage is none of your business—I repeat, none of your business!" She strode off, heels clicking and hair swinging, pushing her way through the throng of people waiting for service near the counter.

"Wow." Ina shook her head. "I think the interview is terminated."

Maggie mulled over the new information. If Meredith had signed a prenuptial agreement, then a divorce would mean that she could only claim certain things from the marital assets. Now that Benton was dead, she'd probably inherited everything. Did Meredith know Benton had found the gold? She had hinted that she knew about Benton's discovery when she'd stopped by the antique shop yesterday, but Maggie had assumed Meredith had been speculating. If not, had that changed Meredith's mind about the divorce—or led to murder?

"Do you mind?" Stella sat in Meredith's chair, not waiting for an invitation. "Sorry about that." She didn't sound at all repentant as she checked out the egg sandwiches. "How are those? I think I'll have one." She reached up an arm and waved at the waitress.

"Are you reporting on Benton's death?" Ina asked, blunt as ever. "That's not your usual fare on *Seacoast Today.*"

"I am." Stella shook back her hair. "I pitched the story to the station manager and he loved it." She thanked the waitress, who brought her a coffee and a promise that her sandwich would be right out. "I have an inside track, you see, since I know the players."

Inserting herself close to the situation also allowed Stella to keep tabs on what was going on. Maggie surprised herself with this cynical thought. One of the worst parts about trying to solve a mystery—especially one where someone has most likely been murdered—was the need to be suspicious of everyone until the culprit was identified. That wasn't her normal mind-set at all.

"When the gold is found, the story will go national and I'll be in the catbird seat. Maybe I can move back to a real network." She shifted her gaze toward Maggie. "Any news on the treasure?"

Maggie flushed, knowing that Stella was needling her about the gold. She tried to sound nonchalant. "Not yet. The ship is docked due to electrical problems."

Stella studied the harbor, where the *Deep Six* sat at anchor. "Since the show is going to continue, I'm sure they'll be going out soon." She leaned back so the waitress could set down her sandwich. "They'd better hurry before someone else scoops it up."

Maggie saw several large boats in the bay. Were any of them treasure hunters?

The reporter took a few bites of sandwich, murmuring appreciation. "Maggie, I was hoping to come over to the shop and film a little today, if that's all right. My crew is here so we might as well do it now."

Maggie put a self-conscious hand to her hair. "I'm not exactly ready."

"Don't worry about it. I can do your makeup. I always do mine when I'm on the road." Stella finished the sandwich in several big bites. "Sorry to eat and run, but I've got to go file my story." She drained her coffee and stood, throwing down a ten-dollar bill. "How does around three o'clock sound?"

"Good, I guess." Maggie wasn't looking forward to it, but to her surprise, she wasn't dreading it either. June would be happy about the free advertising.

"Do you need a PA?" Ina asked. "I'm real cheap. Like free."

Stella studied Ina's hat, clearly amused. "Why not?"

"Goody. I get to work on another show." Ina rubbed her hands together with glee.

"See you later, ladies." Stella bolted for the door, and as she went out, Robert Linton entered. At the sight of the officer, the volume of conversation dipped for a moment, then rose again. Robert stood gazing around the room, and when Daisy popped out of the kitchen, he approached her.

From where they sat, Maggie couldn't hear what he said, but she had a clear view of the reaction his words caused. Daisy swayed, and before Robert could catch her, she slumped to the floor.

15

A crowd of curious and concerned people quickly surrounded Daisy, lying prone on the floor next to the counter.

Maggie and Ina jumped up, pressing forward through the onlookers to reach their friend. By the time they got there, Daisy was sitting up with Robert hunkered beside her, an arm around her shoulders.

"Let me call an ambulance," Robert said.

"No no. I'm fine." Daisy put a hand to her head. "I fainted for a minute, that's all."

"What's going on?" Ina ducked under a tall man's arm to reach the pair.

Robert's face was white behind the freckles. "I gave her some bad news."

Daisy pulled her knees up and rested her head on her arms. "I'll say."

James appeared at Maggie's side, a welcome sight. "Let's get her into the office." He turned to the rest of the crowd. "Stand back, everyone. Show's over."

The two men helped Daisy up and escorted her to the back of the café, where she had a small office. Maggie and Ina followed. The room contained a desk, two chairs, and a couple of file cabinets, and after the five of them squeezed inside, Maggie could barely close the door. Daisy sat behind the desk and the rest of them stood.

"I take it there's news about Benton's death." James crossed his arms and leaned against the wall.

Robert fidgeted, shuffling from one foot to the other. "Yes, there is. I wanted to tell Daisy before . . . before they take the next step."

"Spit it out, Robert." Ina's tone was scolding, and Maggie imagined her speaking the same way to her nephew when he was a boy.

Robert pulled off his hat and brushed a hand through his short hair. "It's definitely murder. The autopsy revealed a stab wound."

"A stab wound?" Maggie hadn't expected to hear that. She thought maybe Benton was pushed and hit his head. "That's what killed him?"

"Appears so. There wasn't any water in his lungs, so he wasn't breathing when he went in." Robert settled his hat back on his head. "Unfortunately they're still looking at Harry as the primary suspect."

Daisy moaned, her head in her hands. "I can't believe this. Harry and Benton fought, but Harry didn't stab him!"

"It's that darn button, Daisy," Robert said. "It's a match for Harry's coat. They figure the assailant and Benton struggled, and when Benton fell into the water, he took the button with him."

"So what's next, Robert?" James asked.

"They have a warrant out for Harry's arrest." When Daisy opened the desk drawer and pulled out her purse, Robert guessed what she was thinking. "Don't bother trying to reach him first, Daisy. We've already got officers waiting for him to come in from pulling traps." He hitched up his belt. "I suggest that you call a lawyer, and it should probably be one who specializes in criminal defense."

. . . .

Maggie knew she would never forget the scene when Harry Carter pulled his lobster boat into its berth only to find the police waiting—and the media watching. She and Ina were also there, supporting Daisy, who insisted on being present.

Harry took the news of his arrest for murder with good grace, ducking his head as Robert Linton read him his rights while another officer fastened the cuffs on his wrists. "Take care of the boat and the catch—and my wife," Harry called to his overalls-clad helper, who watched in shock from the deck of the *Daisy Mae.*

Maggie slipped an arm around Daisy's shoulders. "We'll take care of you too."

Daisy drew Ina into the hug on the other side. "I'm so grateful for my friends."

. . . .

"Come on in, Robert. I appreciate you stopping by." After getting home from The Busy Bean, Maggie had called the station and reported the theft of Abigail's papers. Much to her surprise, Robert arrived within a few minutes of her call.

"I'm happy to have the break, to be honest." Robert shook his head. "Tough day when you arrest one of your friends." He took off his hat and set it on the hall table.

"Would you like coffee? There's a fresh pot." Maggie led the way to the kitchen.

"I wouldn't say no to a cup." Robert settled in the breakfast nook, giving Snickers a scratch behind the ears.

Maggie served the coffee along with fixings, as Daisy would put it, and set out a plate of homemade oatmeal cookies. "Help yourself."

"Thanks, I will." Robert took a cookie. "I haven't eaten much today."

"I can make you a sandwich." Maggie jumped back up. "I've got turkey and Swiss."

"That's awfully nice, Maggie." Robert settled back, continuing to pat Snickers while he drank his coffee.

"Mayo or mustard?" Maggie pulled whole-grain bread from the bread box.

"Mayo, please." Robert took out his pad and pen. "Tell me about what was stolen."

"Someone took a small trunk containing Abigail Sedgwick's papers from the backseat of my car." Anticipating his question, she added, "It happened sometime after the historical society meeting a couple of nights ago. I discovered it was missing late last night after I got back from the Carters' house."

"Car unlocked the whole time?"

"Yes, I believe so. It was in the driveway until I drove over to the Carters. I didn't lock the car there either." Maggie set the plate holding a sandwich and kettle-style potato chips in front of Robert.

Robert picked up a sandwich half and took a bite, then wiped his mouth with a napkin. "Good sandwich. Anything of value in the trunk?"

Maggie sat down and picked up her mug. "Only to me. Of course there was information about the shipwreck in there and Abigail's journal. We found a letter from Lemuel Jenkins, an ancestor of Clem's. You know, the old grump who hangs around at the docks."

"I know Clem. So you think the theft has something to do with the shipwreck?"

"I can't think of any other reason. The only people who would find the trunk valuable would be the historical society members, and they wouldn't have any cause to steal it. "

"True." Robert made a note. "Well, I'll see what I can do. We'll notify the pawnshops and other antiques dealers in case someone tries to sell the trunk."

"I appreciate that." Secretly Maggie believed that someone interested in the shipwreck had taken the papers, either to learn something or to prevent her from doing so. "While you're checking the other shops, can you find out if one of them sold a carved wooden box?" She gestured. "About this big. Someone left one full of white feathers on the doorstep of the shop. Probably the same person who left the skeleton."

"Another prank, you think?" Robert tossed a chip into his mouth, then picked up the second half of his sandwich. Almost as quickly, he set the sandwich down again and snapped his fingers. "Maybe the trunk theft was a prank too."

"Could be." She doubted it, but if he wanted to pursue that theory, then they might find out who was leaving the unpleasant items. She allowed Robert to finish his sandwich in peace before changing the subject. "You don't believe Harry is guilty, do you?"

Robert grimaced. "I really can't discuss the particulars with you, Maggie. The chief would kill me. You know that."

"It was worth a shot." Maggie got up and retrieved the coffeepot. "Refill?"

"Sure, I'll take a warm-up."

She topped off his mug. "There are a lot of people who had issues with Benton. Harry's is the thinnest reason of all—that he was angry at him for mouthing off."

Robert poured cream into his brew. "All right. If you believe that, fill me in."

"Let's see. We've got Meredith Lee, who likely signed a prenuptial agreement and stood to lose a lot if they got divorced, especially if they find gold. Rory James, who was Benton's rival. Even Stella Marquez, who knew Benton in Hollywood and, according to her, helped him get started in the business. Lately he's been refusing to help her. Who knows who else?

Oh yes, Kristen, the sound girl. She's involved with someone in the crew. Maybe it was Benton."

Robert chuckled. "What a soap opera. Are you sure you're not making up all this drama?"

Maggie had to admit it did sound like a potboiler plot. But rivalry, love, and money were all motives for murder. "I'd prefer to think it's one of them rather than Harry."

"True. Too true." Robert stared into space. "You know, I probably shouldn't tell you this, but the murder weapon is tied to Somerset Harbor."

Maggie's pulse leaped. "You found it? It wasn't tossed into the water?" Had the weapon, like the coat, been directly traceable to Harry?

"I don't doubt it's at the bottom of the harbor. I was referring to the size and shape of the wound. Doc believes it was made by a whaling lance." He demonstrated the approximate size. "They were used to kill whales after they were harpooned."

"But people haven't whaled here in decades!"

"That's right. But there are a lot of those old fishing tools hanging around. People don't use them, but they don't get rid of them either." He frowned. "Harry's bait shed is full of them."

Maggie thought of someone else who was a pack rat. "What about Clem Jenkins? He's got tons of junk at his house. And his ancestor was on the *Abigail*. He's still bitter about it."

"Old Clem? Sorry, Maggie. I can't see it." He sighed and dropped his crumpled napkin on his empty plate. "But I can't see Harry doing it either."

· · · · · · · · · · · · · · · · ·

"How does this look, Maggie?" June made a final tweak to the display of maritime items she'd put together for the television shoot, helped by Ina, their PA for the day.

"It looks wonderful, June." Maggie was sincere in her praise. June had created a cozy nook using a fireplace mantel that was for sale. Above it hung the painting of a ship at sea and a mariner's clock. On a gateleg table flanked by two Windsor chairs were the nautical chart, sextant, captain's hat, and spyglass.

Something new was featured on the table too, a burl-wood box with ivory inlay around the edge. "What's that?" Maggie asked.

"It's a lap desk. Captains often used them."

The bells on the shop door jingled, and Stella entered, followed by a man carrying a camera. "Here we are, Maggie. Are you ready for us?"

Maggie smoothed her black pencil skirt. "I think so."

"Great." Stella directed her cameraman where to set up, and Ina was assigned to help with plugging in cords and arranging lamps so the lighting was bright enough.

Setting a latched case on the counter, Stella peered at Maggie's face. "You only need a little foundation and rouge so you don't look washed out. I like the way you did your eyes." She began to pull items out of the case.

"Thanks. I copied what Daisy did for the first shoot at the mansion."

Stella's hand paused in midair. "Daisy Carter? They arrested her husband, right?" She gave Maggie a sly glance. "She a friend of yours?"

Irritation flared as Maggie sensed where Stella was going. "She is, but I'm not going to be your go-between for an interview. Don't even ask."

Stella shrugged. "It was worth a try. Have a seat and I'll fix you up."

As the reporter worked on her face, Maggie tried to tamp down her annoyance. She was doing this for the shop, and she needed to keep her focus on that.

"I don't think he did it," Stella announced as she dabbed at Maggie's face with a damp sponge.

"That makes two of us," Maggie said, careful not to move her cheeks too much while she spoke. "Four if you count June and Ina." June was talking to the camera operator and Ina by the display.

"I mean, Harry barely knew Benton, so why would he kill him?" Stella set the foundation cake aside and picked up rouge.

"I totally agree. Benton had been a little flirtatious with Daisy, but I don't think Harry is the jealous type."

Stella leaned a little closer, lowering her voice. "Benton was. And he didn't like the, ah, *close friendship* that was blossoming between Rory and Meredith."

Maggie had wondered about their relationship too, after witnessing their covert discussion in the Sedgwick Manor hallway and the late-night stroll along the shore path. But she bit her tongue, not wanting to add fuel to the fire. It was bad enough one person was being falsely accused.

Stella tipped up Maggie's chin. "Smile. That's it. You're beautiful." She snapped the rouge container shut and discarded the sponge.

"Thanks, I appreciate it." Maggie squinted at the reflection of herself in a nearby mirror. Her makeup did look good.

Stella started the filming with a short introduction. "I'm so glad you could join me today in the lovely coastal town of Somerset Harbor. This delightful little fishing village has a long and storied history."

She paused, presumably for effect. When she continued, her voice was foreboding. "Including being the site of the famous wreck of the *Abigail*. Oh, there have been many wrecks along the Maine coast, but one thing sets the wreckage of the *Abigail* apart: It is rumored to hold the spoils of a bank robbery." She smiled, and her tone warmed. "I'm visiting with Maggie Watson, whose family tree includes the *Abigail*'s captain, Thomas Sedgwick. Maggie runs an antiques shop on the grounds of Sedgwick Manor, the ancestral home Thomas built for his wife, who was named—you guessed it—Abigail."

The camera panned the interior of the shop as Stella continued, "Carriage House Antiques has a wonderful assortment of vintage and valuable items. Maggie has put together a display of nautical items related to Maine's maritime history."

Maggie threw June a grimace at this last statement since June had done all the work on the vignette.

June smiled and shook her head. "I don't care as long as we get the PR," she whispered.

Stella waved Maggie into the frame, and the next little while was spent discussing each item in the display. Maggie was glad she had listened when June was telling her the provenance and significance of the pieces.

The lap desk was last. "Tell me about this lovely box, Maggie." Stella ran her hand over the satiny finish. "It looks like a lap desk used by captains to store their logs."

"I can't," Maggie said frankly. "I've never seen it before."

Stella threw up a hand. "Cut." The camera operator lowered the camera. "What do you mean?"

June stepped forward. "I found that today and thought I'd include it, since it seemed appropriate. Maggie and I didn't have a chance to talk about it."

"Where did you get it, June?" Maggie lifted the lid flap curiously. The box held an old leather journal, its warped pages revealing it had been soaked at one time. In the back of the lap desk were a couple of drawers.

"It was something Evelyn had in her collection. She said never to sell it but she didn't tell me why."

Maggie explained for the reporter. "My aunt enjoyed mystery and intrigue, Stella." She opened the journal, but the ink had run and some of the pages were stuck together. "I wonder who this belonged to."

June picked up the desk. "Maybe we can figure it out if we study it more closely."

Maggie tugged at the tiny drawers but they didn't open. "I guess they're stuck."

Stella gave a yip of excitement. "I bet they're false." She opened a second lid, on the raised area at the rear of the box. Underneath was a scooped-out length flanked by two small square storage areas.

"A place to put pens and inkwells," June said.

"That's right. Watch." Stella pressed on one side of the scooped area, which lifted and came out, revealing a space underneath. Ina and the camera operator crowded close to see what was inside.

"It's empty." Maggie felt a stab of disappointment.

Stella grinned at her. "Don't be disappointed yet." She lifted off the entire back to display another open area. "This is why the drawers don't work. They front this hidden storage area."

"There's something in there," June said. "Go ahead, Maggie, it belongs to you."

Maggie reached inside and pulled out a small black velvet pouch. It smelled musty, as if it had been wet at one time. She squeezed it and felt something hard inside.

"Open it, open it." Stella jumped up and down with glee. "We're going to have to stage this again on camera. It's too good."

Gently tugging on the top, Maggie eased open the pouch and tipped it so the contents would slide out. "It's a gold pocket watch."

"May I?" June asked.

At Maggie's nod, she picked it up and opened the metal lid covering the watch dial.

"A hunter case watch. The crystal is still intact." June flipped it over and squinted at the engraving. "Maggie." Her voice shook. "I think this watch belonged to Thomas Sedgwick."

16

June handed the watch to Maggie, who took it with trembling fingers. The inscription read, *To Thomas, from your beloved Abigail.*

Maggie glanced at the damaged journal. "Does that mean that's his ship's log?"

"It could very well be." June opened the book again and squinted at the blurry writing. "I think this lap desk must have washed ashore after the wreck. That's why the book is so heavily water damaged."

"Or someone grabbed it when the ship was sinking," Stella said. "They might have thought it contained something valuable."

Maggie imagined sailors—or the Confederate thieves—grabbing what they could as the ship broke apart against the rocks. She ran her fingers along the glossy top of the lap desk. *If only it could speak.*

June continued to leaf through the journal. "This has to be the ship's log. Look at this entry, talking about sailing out of New York." She handed the book to Maggie.

"You're right." With rising excitement, Maggie went to the back and flipped forward. Then she groaned in disappointment. "Oh no. There are pages missing." She held up the book so the others could see. Several pages at the back had been torn out, leaving only rough edges to show where they had been. "I bet those entries detailed the last voyage." Her heart sank. Had those pages proved the captain's innocence? Or had they implicated him?

....

Home at last, Maggie made one of her comfort food meals, macaroni and cheese served with stewed tomatoes on the side. She built a toasty fire in the library and then settled down to eat and watch the news. Snickers wedged himself into the armchair beside her. Stella had promised that the segment with her would be part of a special report.

The Portland news broadcast opened with Benton's murder. Stella gave the commentary, standing on the docks with her hair blowing in the breeze while Harry was being led away by the police. The standard expression of shock regarding murder in such a quaint Maine town was offered, then the camera cut to shots of the mansion and the antiques shop.

Maggie's cell rang, and she set aside her plate and picked it up. *Emily.* "Hey, hon."

"Mom! Are you watching the news?" Emily's voice rose to a pitch that reminded Maggie of when she was little and something exciting was happening.

"Yes, I am." The shot on the TV cut to Stella in the antiques shop giving her introduction. "I'm on in a sec." Still holding the phone but not talking, Maggie watched the show, conscious that her daughter was also viewing.

Rather than the full discussion of the other maritime items, the clip focused on the discovery of the ship's log and watch in the lap desk. Stella had staged the discovery for the camera, and it was effectively done.

"That's so exciting," Emily said. "You found Captain Sedgwick's watch and logbook?"

"We did," Maggie said. "Unfortunately the entry page from the day of the wreck was ripped out."

"Hmm. That's weird." Emily giggled as Ina appeared on-screen, studying the watch. "I love Ina's hat."

At the end of the segment, Stella blindsided Maggie when she asked, "Do you think the *Deep Sea Secrets* crew will find the gold?" Both she and Maggie knew the answer to that.

Maggie wasn't good at lying, but as she struggled to find

something to say, Ina piped up, "If they do or if they don't, we know one thing: Thomas Sedgwick was innocent, and so is Harry Carter."

"I adore Ina," Emily said. "She's so feisty and funny."

"Me too." Maggie had been relieved by Ina's quick thinking.

"Only time will tell on both counts," Stella concluded. She then gave a pitch for her show, which would feature the other antiques and an "in-depth interview" with Maggie Watson. The news went to something else, and Maggie muted the volume.

"You looked great, Mom," Emily said. "Is it fun being on television? I wish I could come down while you're shooting, but all my professors collaborated to make sure I'm too busy."

"It's okay. How's school going?" Maggie shifted the conversation to her daughter, and they chatted a few minutes longer. After they hung up, she tuned back in to catch the weather. A northeaster was headed their way, due to strike in two days—if it didn't blow out to sea.

Maggie hoped the storm would indeed blow itself out. They needed to get that gold off the ocean floor fast. And she needed to find the missing pages of the log or the other evidence Evelyn had mentioned. She would send the figurehead to be x-rayed in the morning, she decided.

Her cell phone rang again. Daisy was on the line. "Any news, Daisy?"

"Yes. Do you think you could come to the bail hearing late tomorrow morning? I could really use your support." She sniffled, and Maggie realized she was crying. "Sam Skyler is away so we're getting another district attorney. And word on the street is that he goes for the jugular."

. . . .

Maggie hurried up the sidewalk to the municipal building, where the bail hearing was to be held. Daisy, June, Ruth, and Liz were clustered near the steps waiting for her. Everyone exchanged hugs, then as the clock on the tower moved to five before eleven, they trooped up the stairs.

"Did the defense attorney show up?" Maggie asked. Evelyn's estate lawyer had recommended Walt Waystack for Harry's defense, and fortunately he had been available.

"Yes, he's already inside." Daisy held the door open for her friends. "He looks like a tough one, thank goodness."

The municipal courtroom was located on the second floor, so they climbed the main staircase and went through a set of tall double doors. Proceedings involving adults charged with certain felonies were public in Maine, but Maggie was still surprised by the size of the audience.

"Big news for Somerset Harbor," June whispered as they slid onto a bench near the front.

"For everywhere, apparently," Maggie whispered back. Reporters, including Stella Marquez, were scattered throughout the room. No television cameras, though—those weren't allowed. The defense attorney did look tough. Although not terribly tall, he had an eager look and the pointed nose of a hound scenting prey.

"All rise," the bailiff intoned, and everyone in the courtroom stood as the judge entered.

Daisy groaned at the sight of the rotund, red-faced man dressed in a long black robe seating himself at the bench. "He's rumored to be harsh," she whispered.

The judge struck his gavel to start the hearing. The tall and cadaverous district attorney made a case in a plummy Boston Brahmin accent that Harry should be denied bail because he was a flight risk.

Walt Waystack jumped in. "Harry Carter has been a resident of this community all his life, Your Honor. He has a wife, children, a business. He won't leave them behind."

"But he's a fisherman, Your Honor," the prosecutor said. "He can get in his boat and flee to Canada with ease. He's facing a charge of first-degree murder, and that could mean life without parole."

First-degree murder. That meant the prosecutor believed that Harry had planned the murder. Maggie assumed it must have been the use of a whaling lance that clinched it. Those weren't exactly pocket items.

Daisy squeezed Maggie's hand hard. On Daisy's other side, Liz bowed her head in prayer, also holding Daisy's hand.

The judge eyed Harry for a long moment. Harry stood with dignity, returning the judge's gaze with his head held high. The judge finally nodded and rapped his gavel again, declaring that Harry could post surety for his bail, meaning a lien on his property, including the boat. "You are ordered to refrain from pulling traps until after trial, Mr. Carter."

Harry had made bail, but he wouldn't be able to engage in his livelihood.

"What will he do?" Liz asked Daisy.

"He'll have to hire a second helper and send them out," Daisy said. Tears streamed down her face. "I'm so thankful he's coming home."

"We're going to make sure this case never makes it to trial. Right, ladies?" June's mouth was a grim line.

"That's right." Maggie hardened her resolve. They had to find the real killer.

A short while later, Liz, June, and Maggie parted ways in front of the municipal building. Daisy was waiting inside for Harry to be processed and released.

"See you later," Liz said. "I'm going over to the church." Old Faith Chapel was on the next block of Monroe Avenue. She waved and walked off.

"I'm headed for the shop," June said, jingling her keys. "Want a ride, Maggie?"

"I think I'll walk since it's such a nice day." The sky was so blue and the air so clear it was hard to believe a storm was coming. A "weather breeder," Ina and other old-timers called it. "But I'll be over at the shop this afternoon."

"See you then." June jumped into her car and sped away.

Maggie took her time strolling along the streets, enjoying the opportunity to think while drinking in the ocean view. So much had happened over the past few days—it was all whirling around in her head. Once again she went through the catalog of suspects. Fortunately, she had a good excuse to talk to most of them since she was on the show.

There was one person she hadn't spoken to lately. Clem Jenkins. With his family history, he was dead set against the salvage operation. Had he been angry enough to strike out at Benton? She would wager that he owned a whaling lance or two.

Then again, the same could be said for many men from Somerset Harbor.

Almost without volition, Maggie found her steps moving toward the harbor. Come to think of it, she hadn't seen Clem since before Benton's death. Why hadn't he been among the onlookers when Benton was pulled from the water? He only lived a short distance from there. Surely he should have been there, spouting his nonsense about jinxes and curses.

Unless he was guilty and had fled . . .

Maggie was almost running by the time she reached Clem's shanty. Everything was quiet in the still air, the only sound small waves shushing on the pebbled shore. A seagull launched itself from Clem's roof with a squawk as she approached.

She knocked on the front door's windowpane, then jumped in surprise when her fist made the door swing open. Both concerned and curious, she pushed the door open farther and stuck her head inside. "Clem? Clem, are you home?"

No answer. With all the curtains drawn, the stuffy room was nearly dark. But Maggie saw enough to realize something.

The place had been torn apart.

17

Clem owned a lot of stuff and he wasn't terribly organized. Maggie had noticed that when she last visited. But now his home held the vibrations of violence, revealed by the sofa cushions, books flung all over the floor, and pictures hanging askew, one of the frames broken.

And where was Clem?

"Clem, are you here?" Maggie called out. "Are you hurt?" Treading carefully so as to avoid broken glass, she picked her way through the small main room, which served as living room, dining room, and kitchen. Off to one side was a tiny bedroom and bathroom, both deserted.

Maggie's heart slowed in relief when she realized the old man was gone, not lying injured—or worse. To double-check her theory, she went outside to the open shed behind the house. She had spotted a pickup truck there last time. It, too, was gone.

Had Clem left under his own steam? Had he killed Benton and run away? If so, who had trashed his house? *Too many questions.* Maggie pulled out her cell phone and called Robert Linton. Then she sat on the front porch and waited.

"What brings you to Clem's, Maggie?" Robert asked as he strolled around the corner of the house, adjusting his belt.

"I came down here to ask Clem some questions and noticed that his house has been vandalized. And he's gone." Maggie led the way to the front door, which she pushed open for Robert.

"Hmm. It does look bad. Not that Clem is a neat freak at the best of times." Robert scratched the back of his head. "Some kids must have gotten in here." He made a note.

"You don't seem very worried. What if something bad happened to him?"

Robert raised one brow. "Like what? He was kidnapped?" He chuckled. "Someone is holding him for ransom, maybe? Old Clem doesn't have two nickels to rub together."

"Maybe he killed Benton. Or knows who did." Maggie found herself gesturing wildly, trying to convince her officer friend that the situation was serious. The hollow feeling gnawing in her belly told her something was wrong.

"I highly doubt it." Officer Linton shook his head. "I'm thinking Clem went on a trip, and someone took advantage of his absence and had a little party in here."

Maggie crossed her arms. "Can't you put out an APB on his truck or something?"

Robert chuckled again. "No, I can't do that. I don't have any probable cause. There's no sign of foul play here. Just a big fat mess."

Maggie fumed all the way to the shop, the only benefit of her anger the fast pace she maintained even striding uphill. She really appreciated Robert, who had helped her more times than she could count. But sometimes he had an unfortunate blind spot. Right now that blind spot was shared by the entire Somerset Harbor police force, with their focus on the case against Harry.

Reaching the shop at last, she burst through the front door, startling June.

"There you are. I was about to call you." June waved her cell phone in demonstration. "Did you take the lap desk home last night?"

"No, I didn't." Puffing, Maggie sagged down onto a conveniently placed Queen Anne armchair. A spring poked her behind and she made a mental note to have James fix it. "Why do you ask?"

"It's gone. I didn't notice right away since it wasn't on display. But when I went into the back room, I thought I'd take another look at it." June began to pace about the shop, peering high and low as though the precious item were hiding.

Maggie put a hand to her head. "You're kidding. Someone broke in here and stole it?" *How did they know—oh yes* . . . After the news broadcast, everyone in Maine knew about the lap desk. Why hadn't she stored it somewhere safe? She should have at least taken the watch that was tucked inside it home.

June returned to the counter and picked up her phone again. "I'd better call the police and report the break-in."

"We might as well set up a direct hotline to Robert," Maggie said. "I saw him half an hour ago. I'll tell you about it when you finish the call." An awful thought struck her, and she launched herself out of the chair, hurrying to the back room.

She sagged in relief when she spotted the figurehead still standing in the corner. "I'm sending you away today," she told the wooden woman. "Before you vanish too."

The rest of the afternoon was a flurry of activity, with the police arriving to take a statement about the stolen lap desk and James helping to package the figurehead for shipment. He put together a special wooden crate, and the bubble-wrapped statue was carefully swaddled in moving blankets and securely fastened inside. A driver came to deliver it to an art conservator's facility in Boston, where the figurehead would be x-rayed.

Maggie was drinking coffee with June and James and telling them about Clem's disappearance when Rory called. The reality show team was having a dinner meeting and she was invited.

· · · · · · · · · · · · · · · · ·

"I'm in charge now and what I say goes. Got it?"

At the sound of Rory's angry voice, Maggie paused outside the conference room. The desk clerk had directed her to the room, saying that their meal would be served during a working meeting. *Should I leave?* She hated to intrude upon a private argument.

With a sigh, Maggie squared her shoulders and turned the doorknob. She was an invited guest, and they could ask her not to come in if necessary. Besides, she needed to know what was going on so she could help Harry.

She saw Rory and Captain Gene facing off when she entered the room, both men red-faced and glaring.

"I can't let you put my men at risk," Captain Gene said. He grabbed a roll from the breadbasket and broke it apart with his thick fingers. "Not even for TV." He popped a piece in his mouth and chewed.

Rory whirled to face her at the sound of the door clicking shut. His face smoothed itself out, and his voice had lost its edge when he spoke. "Hi, Maggie. Glad you could make it. Help yourself to food." He gestured toward a table against the wall where containers were laid out. The rest of the group—Addison, Chris, Kristen, and the computer techs—were seated with the captain and Rory around a long table.

"Maybe Maggie has an opinion," Captain Gene said as she moved to the table and began serving herself salad, ham, and roasted vegetables. "This joker wants to send an inflatable raft out in a storm to get footage."

"I'm not the person to ask," Maggie said. She found an empty seat next to Addison, who greeted her with a nod. "Kristen, can you please pass me the water pitcher?" The young woman cheerfully granted Maggie's request. She appeared better rested and more cheerful today, which was probably evidence that Benton hadn't been her secret romantic partner.

"We need drama," Rory said. "Drama! That's an area that I know a lot about." He thrust out his muscled forearms. "I've wrestled crocodiles and handled snakes. All very safe, but the viewers didn't need to know that."

"How would we film such a thing?" Chris asked. "From the deck of the *Deep Six*? We'd need a good zoom for that."

"I'm thinking those action cameras. You know, the ones you wear on your head?" Rory demonstrated. "They make them waterproof."

Maggie pictured shots of lashing rain and huge waves rising and falling while the crew fought to keep the boat upright. Dramatic, all right, but also very dangerous.

"Do you really think we'll get a storm?" Addison changed the subject. "Today was incredibly clear and calm. Lovely day."

"If the usual weather pattern holds true, then yes," Maggie said. "I've seen it before."

"If you don't like the weather in Maine, wait a minute," Chris quipped.

Fortunately for the group's digestion, Rory dropped the topic of extreme filming and they ate in silence for a few minutes.

Addison turned to Maggie. "I've been meaning to call you. I located some very interesting paperwork regarding Thomas Sedgwick's business affairs."

It was on the tip of her tongue to ask if he had found it in Abigail's trunk, but Maggie restrained herself. No sense in antagonizing the professor, or anyone else for that matter.

"I'd love to see it." She forced a smile.

Addison turned away from the table and rummaged in a leather satchel, pulling out a letter in a clear plastic sleeve. "This is only a copy. The original is in a university library collection in Massachusetts." He handed it to her with a smirk.

The handwritten letter was on stationery with a bank name

printed on the top. With a start, Maggie recognized the institution as the one the Confederates had targeted. The letter, addressed to Captain Thomas Sedgwick, made a demand that funds be paid on a loan immediately. The letter was dated a couple of weeks before the robbery.

"I've looked into that bank, and they were known for unfair business practices." Addison's tone was smug. "Maybe that's why Sedgwick steered his Confederate comrades toward that particular one."

Maggie was outraged. "There is no evidence that Thomas steered anyone. He was an innocent bystander." She waved the letter. "This is a coincidence."

Addison smirked as he picked up his fork. "Tell yourself that, my dear. I might if I were in your shoes." He winked as he took a dainty bite of ham.

The man was infuriating. Appetite gone, Maggie laid her utensils across her half-finished meal. "How are the repairs going on the boat?" she asked Captain Gene. She'd rather risk hearing one of his awful jokes than talk to the professor further.

"Pretty good," the captain said. "We were fortunate the damage was contained so quickly."

"When do you think we can go out again?" Rory asked. "Tomorrow, maybe?"

Gene shook his head. "Probably not. I don't think the repairs will be done until the day after."

Rory plucked his bottom lip. "Great, just great. Every day we delay is costing us money." He pushed back his chair and grabbed his cell. "I'd better call the network and tell them what's up." The new host of *Deep Sea Secrets* stomped from the room, leaving an uneasy silence in his wake.

"Ugh, what a tyrant he's turning out to be," Chris said after Rory was safely out of earshot.

Kristen gave a little moan. "I miss Benton."

"He was easier to work for," one of the techs said. "That's for sure."

"'Uneasy lies the head that wears a crown,'" Addison said, quoting Shakespeare. He wiped his mouth with his napkin, eyeing the food table. "Who wants dessert?"

Maggie excused herself, planning to go home for an early night. She was longing for some alone time to digest all that had happened, not to mention her interrupted dinner. Her stomach ached from the tension in the room.

The hotel featured a small flower shop, and as she passed the display of fall bouquets, she had an idea. First she stopped by the desk. "Can you please tell me if Meredith Lee is in?" she asked the clerk.

"I'll check for you." The clerk picked up the phone. "Who shall I say is calling?"

"Maggie Watson." Maggie glanced around the lobby while she waited, enjoying the hotel's elegant but comfortable ambiance. A couple walked hand in hand toward the grand staircase, and Maggie smiled when she recognized Kristen and Eric, one of the computer techs. That was one mystery solved. Maggie wished the couple well as they began to climb the staircase, still holding hands.

"You can go right up," the clerk said. "Room 301." She pointed. "The elevator is around the corner."

Maggie thanked her. Before going upstairs, she made a detour to the flower shop. She'd be more welcome bearing gifts, she was sure. Then she headed up to Meredith's room and knocked on the door.

Meredith opened it. "Maggie! Come on in." She stood back to let Maggie enter. "Are those for me? You shouldn't have." She beamed despite her protest, burying her nose in the bright flowers as she carried the vase to the mahogany table by the window. Room 301 was a spacious suite, with a sitting room and a bedroom. Like the rest of the hotel, the furniture was Victorian in style but new and expensive reproductions rather than antiques.

"I couldn't resist," Maggie said. "They were so pretty." Following Meredith's lead, she sat on one of the love seats. "I wanted to stop in for a minute and see how you're doing."

Meredith plucked a tissue from a box on the side table and clutched it in one fist. "Tell you what, honey, I've been better." Her Southern accent was a warm blur.

Maggie leaned forward, wishing she could hug Meredith but feeling constrained by their brief acquaintance. "I know how you feel." When Meredith glanced up sharply, she added, "I really do know. I lost my husband a few years ago."

"I'm sorry, sugar. I had no idea." Meredith's eyes welled up. "You're so young." She dabbed at both eyes, sniffing.

"Being in my forties doesn't feel so young a lot of the time." Maggie swallowed. Time was dulling the pain, but now and then it felt fresh. Empathizing with Meredith's loss was bringing it back to life again.

Meredith laughed. "Just a baby. Benton and I were married for over thirty years, believe it or not." She put both hands over her face. "And it's all my fault that he's dead." She burst into tears.

Maggie held her breath, not sure if she could believe her ears. Was Meredith confessing to murder? As the other woman continued to sob, hands over her face, Maggie finally asked, "What do you mean, Meredith?"

Fortunately Meredith's wracking sobs subsided. Scrubbing at her face with the tissue, she opened her mouth to speak. But before she said anything, a key turned in the lock.

Rory entered the suite, frowning when he spotted them. "What's all this?" He hurried to Meredith's side, perching on the sofa and putting an arm around her. He glared at Maggie. "Have you been upsetting her?"

"That wasn't my intention. I brought her some flowers." Maggie sagged back in disappointment, dying to know what Meredith had started to say.

Rory began to croon, whispering endearments to calm Meredith down. After his third glare, Maggie rose to her feet. She obviously wasn't going to learn anything new tonight. One thing was abundantly clear, however. No matter how intense Meredith's grief was for her late husband, she and Rory were much more than friends.

"I'll leave you be," she said, heading for the door. She paused, hand on the handle. "Congratulations on your new role as host, Rory." Her intent was innocent, a polite acknowledgement of his promotion.

Rory didn't take it that way. Leaving Meredith's side, he jumped to his feet. "What do you mean by that, lady?" Both of his large hands were clenched into tight fists.

Maggie backed up against the door. "Nothing. I was merely being polite. I mean, they could have pulled the plug, right? Instead they offered the role to you—"

The Aussie advanced on her, forcing her to shrink back even farther. "Are you saying I killed Benton so I could advance in my career?"

Maggie fumbled for the knob. "Of course not. I was being nice." Finally it turned in her sweaty hand, and she pulled the door open.

Rory pushed at his already-rolled-up sleeves, one arm, then the other. "I think we're all done here, Maggie. Going forward, we won't need you on the show."

Meredith gasped. "Rory! That's not necessary. Maggie is a great addition."

"I don't care. I don't need people snooping around, interfering with my management of the show."

It took a moment for Rory's words to sink in. "You're firing me? But what about the contract?"

Rory folded his arms. "We'll pay you for what you've done so far, of course."

It wasn't about the money — it was access to the salvage operation that mattered to her. But Maggie couldn't say that. She swallowed, managing to say past the lump in her throat, "As you wish. Good night."

She escaped, practically running down the quiet hallway, cheeks flaming. She'd never been fired from anything in her life. Reaching the elevator, she pushed the button. What had set him off? Reviewing her comments, she couldn't find anything. So why was he pushing her away?

There could only be one reason. *Guilt.*

Maggie retrieved her keys from the valet and emerged from the hotel into the cool evening air. A breeze carrying the odor of salt lifted her hair. On an impulse, she decided to walk down to the shore and check on Clem. Maybe he was back from wherever he had gone. The scene with Rory and Meredith fresh in her mind, she now thought that Clem might have been a witness rather than the culprit. He was always lurking around. Maybe he had seen something important.

The shore path was lit well enough that Maggie found her way easily to the end, where the humble houses sat along the shore. In a few, lights were on, and the blue flickering of televisions revealed that their occupants were snuggled in for the night. At Clem's, the house was dark. But as she watched, a light came on in the lean-to shed in the back. *He must be home.*

Around the back of his house, it was pitch-dark except for the meager light shining from the shed. Despite shuffling slowly and her best efforts to avoid obstacles, Maggie tripped on a rock and stumbled forward with a cry. Fortunately, she regained her balance before she fell flat. Then she had a bright idea. Her cell phone had a flashlight function. Digging it out of her bag, she scrolled through the applications and turned it on. The thin blue light was better than nothing.

"Clem?" she called as she got closer to the half-open door, holding up her phone. "Are you there?"

No one answered. Maggie crossed the last few feet of lumpy, overgrown grass. Maybe he had come and gone again, leaving the light on by accident.

"Clem?" she called again.

Maggie felt something shove her back, propelling her forward into the shed. Her cell phone flew out of her hand.

The door slammed behind her, and she heard the unmistakable sound of a padlock clicking shut. She was trapped.

18

A hollow silence followed the click of the lock. It took a moment for Maggie to fully comprehend the situation, but then she launched herself at the door, pounding it with her fists. "Let me out! Let me out now!" She screamed on and on until she thought her voice would give out.

No answer. Maggie's fists stung from the contact with the rough wood, and her throat hurt. What in the world was she going to do?

Her cell phone was outside somewhere, so she couldn't call for help. Panic swirled in her belly and rose up into her throat. How long would it be before someone realized she was missing and found her? It could be days, weeks . . . She pictured someone finding her skeleton. She'd become another Somerset Harbor legend—the missing heiress of Sedgwick Manor.

Maggie screamed again, this time in fear and frustration. Then with a huge effort, she calmed herself. Getting out of here was up to her. Emily and Snickers were counting on her. So were Daisy and Harry, June, James, and her other friends.

In the pale light from a low-watt bulb overhead, she looked around the small space, which smelled of bait, earth, and decaying boards. Old fishing gear, crates, tools, oars, and assorted junk filled most of the square footage. She spotted movement, which made her jump before she realized that she was seeing her reflection in a window blocked by a stack of boxes.

A window. Maybe she could climb out. It took all her strength to shift the boxes, one by one, which felt as if they were filled with lead. Finally, sweating and dirty, she accessed the window.

She regarded it dubiously. It was quite small. She doubted she could fit through it. She pushed on the bottom sash. It wouldn't budge. Probably painted shut or warped so badly it would never open.

A faint ringing drifted to her ears, a melody she recognized. Her cell phone! It was a relief to know it wasn't broken. After a few rings it went silent. If only the person calling would realize there was something wrong. But that wasn't likely. They probably thought she was in bed or in the shower, both of which sounded like heaven right now.

Maggie paced around the tiny area of floor space available, looking for a tool to use. She had to at least try to open the window or, failing that, break the glass. Maybe someone would hear her yelling.

She found a screwdriver and jabbed and scratched at the paint that sealed the sash. Still no luck—it wasn't going to open. *On to Plan B.* Picking up an oar by the paddle end, she tapped the handle on the glass, squeezing her eyes shut. *Bang. Bang. Bang. CRASH!*

Cold fresh air rushed in. She studied the opening. Even if she took out all the broken glass, there was no way she was going to fit through that window.

Taking a deep breath, she yelled, "Help! Help! Someone, help me!"

The night was quiet, the only sound the distant rush of waves. Maggie yelled until she was hoarse. Then she collapsed on an old moldy cushion, exhausted but too keyed up to relax.

Was the person who had locked her in going to come back? At that thought, she jumped up again and grabbed the crowbar. She wasn't going down without a fight.

The bulb overhead flickered, then winked out. *Great.* Now she was in the dark. Something nocturnal skittered in the rafters and she closed her eyes, refusing to look. A mouse? Or something more unpleasant, like a rat?

What a nightmare. She was locked in a tiny, cold, moldy shed, with no apparent chance of escape.

She heard someone laughing outside in the distance. A shaft of light beamed through the window and her heart leapt when she realized it was coming from the shore nearby.

"Help! Help me! I'm trapped!"

The flickering light moved her way, and she could make out voices raised in alarm. Male and female, it sounded like. "Did you hear that? Someone needs help. Where are you?"

"In the shed!" Maggie picked up the oar and thrust it through the broken glass, wiggling it around. "Look for the oar!"

She heard them scrabbling at the lock. "Hold on, we're coming."

Then groans of frustration. "I can't open the padlock."

"What should we do?" the female voice asked.

"I'll go to one of those other houses," the man said. "Maybe someone has some bolt cutters. Stay here, okay?"

"I will. Be careful."

A moment later, Maggie heard footsteps crunching around outside the window. A face appeared on the other side of the unbroken glass. "Hi there."

Maggie recognized the pretty young woman. "Kristen! I'm so glad you're here." *Good thing the young couple had been walking along the shore, or I would have ended up spending the night in this hole.*

"Maggie? How did you end up in there?"

"Long story short, someone pushed me in here and locked the door."

Kristen's mouth dropped open. "Really? That's terrible." She glanced away. "Here comes Eric. Any luck?"

"Yes," Eric called. "The neighbor had a pair of bolt cutters." More rattling at the door, and then it opened.

I'm free! Maggie let out a huge sigh of relief as she hurried out the door to give Kristen and Eric big hugs. "Thank you."

After retrieving her cell phone from the grass, Maggie walked with the couple to return the bolt cutters. She also planned to ask them to escort her back to her car in the hotel parking lot. She'd had enough of walking around alone after dark.

The neighbor was another old salt, a heavy man with a gray crew cut, named Gus. Maggie remembered seeing him around the docks.

"Thanks for letting us use these," Eric said.

"That's all right." Gus took the tool, then scratched his head with his other hand. "What happened?"

"I was locked in Clem's shed," Maggie said. "Someone pushed me inside."

His pale blue eyes widened in alarm. "Pushed you inside? Who would do such a thing? Not Clem."

"No, not Clem. Have you seen him lately?" She might as well take advantage of Gus's attention to ask him a few questions. The young couple stood nearby, listening with interest.

Gus frowned and shook his head. "Not for a few days, actually. Kind of surprised me since Clem is what you'd call a homebody. Never goes anywhere."

"Have you seen anyone else around? Any strangers?"

He chuckled. "There's always strangers around. Have I seen any at Clem's? No, not exactly."

"What do you mean?" Maggie had the sense Gus was enjoying the conversation and trying to prolong it.

"You must have heard someone, not seen them," Eric said shrewdly. Kristen leaned against him, snuggled in the shelter of his arm.

Gus puffed out his lower lip, clearly miffed that Eric had cut to the chase. "That's right. The other night, real late,

Clem was fighting with someone. I couldn't really hear what they said, but it was a whizbang doozy of an argument." He shook his head. "Folks oughta know better than to argue with Clem. He gives as good as he gets, most times. He's a tough old geezer."

Gus must have witnessed Clem's kidnapping without realizing it. Maggie decided to try her luck with one more question. "What night was it?" she asked.

"The night that TV feller got himself killed." Gus began to shut the door. "I'm going to say good night, folks. I'm missing my show."

"What a funny old guy," Eric said as the trio walked along the shore path to the hotel.

"Clem is too," Kristen said. "Isn't he the guy who claimed the shipwreck is jinxed?"

"That's the one." Maggie was beginning to believe him. All the troubles the project had experienced, the ship breakdowns, loss of crew, a fire, their leader murdered . . . But she had the feeling the events were of human origin, not otherworldly. The question remained: Who was behind all this?

"At least they caught the guy who killed Benton," Kristen said. "I never would have guessed it was Harry. He's so nice."

"The jury's still out on that one, Kristen," Eric said before Maggie could protest. "Innocent until proven guilty and all that. Besides, what reason would a lobsterman have to kill Benton? They didn't even know each other."

Upon reflection, Maggie decided to keep quiet. Let the real killer believe that Harry was the scapegoat. Anything she said to these young people would probably be shared.

They reached the parking lot, and Maggie dug her keys out of her purse. "Thanks again for rescuing me. I really appreciate not spending the night in that shed."

"I hope they catch whoever did that to you," Eric said. "That was just plain mean."

Kristen threw herself at Maggie and gave her a hug. "Sleep tight. And see you soon."

Maggie hugged her back. "Have a great night yourself." The young woman's hair smelled like floral shampoo, reminding her of Emily.

"You'll be at the next filming, right?" Eric asked.

Maggie hesitated. Should she tell them? They'd hear about it soon enough. She temporized. "I won't be there. Rory said I wasn't needed." More palatable than saying he'd fired her for accusing him of murder, even if it had been the result of a misunderstanding.

"Ah, too bad." Kristen's mouth pulled down in disappointment. "But we'll see you around town. Maybe we can have coffee at The Busy Bean."

"Sounds good." Maggie jumped into her car, grateful to finally be heading home. The clock on the dash said midnight. She'd been trapped for hours, hours that had seemed like centuries.

· · · · · · · · · · · · · · · · ·

The chime of her cell phone woke Maggie far too early the next morning. Keeping her eyes closed, she fumbled around on the nightstand to locate it. "Hello?"

"Oh, did I wake you? I'm sorry." James was on the line. "I was calling to tell you the figurehead arrived safely in Boston."

Maggie opened one eye. The bedside clock read nine o'clock. No wonder Snickers had been nudging her for an hour. "I guess I slept in." She yawned. "I had a late night."

He chuckled. "Long production meeting? I can't keep up with you television stars."

"Not exactly." It all came back to her in a rush. The contentious meeting. Meredith's tearful confession. Being fired by Rory. Getting locked in Clem's shed. Maggie flung back the covers. "Let me feed Snickers while we talk." She shoved her feet into slippers, grabbed a robe, and shuffled to the kitchen, the "starving" cat on her heels. "Rory fired me last night."

"What? Why would he do that?" James's tone was gratifyingly shocked and angry.

Maggie reached for a can of cat food. "He thought I was accusing him of killing Benton so he could take over the show." She held the phone with her shoulder while she opened the can.

"Huh. Did you?"

She scooped wet food into a clean dish. "Of course not. I was congratulating him on his promotion, and he took it the wrong way."

"Maybe he's guilty."

"That's what I thought."

Snickers attacked the food and began to eat with loud smacking noises. There was no way he was actually starving, and Maggie wondered if he was exaggerating to make a point. Snickers was smart enough to do that.

"You'll never guess what happened next." Maggie paused. "Someone locked me in Clem's shed." She pulled out a bag of fresh-ground coffee from The Busy Bean. No individual pods today—she needed a full pot.

James made an angry exclamation. "Are you all right?"

"I'm fine. It was more scary than dangerous." She took him through the sequence of events. "So, Clem's neighbor heard him fighting with someone before he disappeared. I think Clem might have witnessed the murder. He either took off or was kidnapped."

"Did you call the police? I think you should."

Maggie yawned, wishing that staring at the coffeemaker

would make it drip faster. "Not yet." The front doorbell chimed. "Excuse me, someone's at the door."

"Call me back when you get a chance, okay? And stay out of sheds."

"I'll try." With a laugh, Maggie disconnected. The doorbell chimed again and she hurried to answer, tightening the belt of her robe.

To her surprise, Robert Linton stood on the porch.

"Come on in, Robert. How did you find out about my false imprisonment?"

"False imprisonment? What are you talking about?" Robert's freckled face was a study in puzzlement as he followed Maggie toward the kitchen.

"You don't know? Someone locked me in Clem's shed last night."

He put up a hand. "Hold on. I think I need coffee to hear this."

"Have a seat. I just made some."

Robert slid into the breakfast nook and Maggie poured him a cup. Then she dug out some blueberry muffins with cream cheese frosting and put them out.

"So you didn't come over because of what happened to me last night?" Maggie asked.

"No, and I want to hear all about it. But first I want you to take a look at this." Robert fished a small evidence envelope out of his pocket and slid it across the table to Maggie. "Do you recognize it?"

Maggie picked up the envelope. She certainly did recognize the object. It was one of the earrings she'd sold to Meredith.

19

"This belongs to Meredith Lee," Maggie said, handing the earring back to Robert. "I sold it to her. Where did you find it?"

Robert sipped his coffee. "Down on the docks." He hesitated. "Near where we think Benton went into the water."

"You can tell that?" Maggie's mind raced. Meredith said she blamed herself—had she stabbed Benton and pushed him into the water? She hated to think that; the woman's grief seemed real, but maybe it was tinged with remorse.

"We had a state expert work with us to figure that out. He maps tides and currents to figure out the direction the body moved to end up where it did. That led us to one of the floating docks. We went over it with a fine-tooth comb and voilà."

"Is this going to help Harry?" Maybe the police would admit their mistake and release him.

"I'm afraid I don't know the answer to that." He tucked the plastic bag into his pocket. "But we will talk to Benton's widow and ask her about the earring, see what she has to say." He pulled out his notebook. "So what's this about you and Clem's shed?"

. . . .

"What's the matter, Maggie? You look like something the cat dragged in." June stopped dusting a shelf of glassware to check out her friend.

Maggie sighed as she dropped her handbag behind the counter. "Thanks a lot. But that's exactly how I feel." Once again she launched into a description of her hours in the shed, then backtracked to report that she had been fired from the show.

June set aside her dustcloth and gave Maggie a hug. "I can't believe all that happened between five o'clock last night and this morning. Wow."

"I know. My head is spinning. Oh, I didn't tell you—" Maggie broke off as Meredith Lee entered the shop. She threw June a significant glance, then greeted her customer. "Good morning, Meredith. How are you today?"

The elegant beauty looked as wan and drawn as Maggie felt and—according to June—looked.

Meredith ran a hand through her hair. "I've been better." Her laugh was hollow. "I wanted to apologize for what happened last night." She approached the counter, her bootheels clicking on the hardwood floor. "Rory was really rude to you."

"Do you want coffee?" June mouthed. At Maggie's nod, she disappeared into the back room.

"He's in charge now," Maggie said. "So it's up to him. I won't lie, though, it was a disappointment." She left out the part about being humiliated and upset. What good would it do to air her grievances about Rory?

Meredith, now studying the jewelry display, threw her a sly glance. "There's always Stella's show."

"True." Maggie glanced over her shoulder to make sure June was still out of the room. "To tell you the truth, being on television was June's idea. She saw it as free advertising for the shop."

"It sure would be." Meredith's gaze focused on the earrings. "Can I see those?" She pointed to a pair of sapphire-and-diamond drops.

"Back for another purchase?" Maggie deliberately kept her voice innocent as she unlocked the cabinet. "How are the other ones working out for you?" She wasn't going to mention that the police had found one in case it interfered with their investigation.

Meredith shook her head. "You won't believe it, but I lost one. Already."

Maggie paused in the act of setting out the black velvet cloth. "Really? That's too bad." She reached down and pulled out the pair of earrings, carefully watching Meredith's face.

Meredith bit her lip. "I know, so careless of me. And of course I've been walking along the shore, so it could be anywhere."

"Oh yes, if you drop something on the rocks you'll never find it." *Or on the docks.* Maggie placed the earrings so they displayed well. "Aren't these beautiful?"

June bustled out of the back room, balancing three mugs of coffee in her hands. "I brought you one, Meredith, just in case."

"How thoughtful." Meredith blinked away tears as she reached for the mug. "People here are so nice."

June threw Maggie a concerned look. "I'll go get sugar and milk."

Meredith took a sip. "None for me, thanks. I take mine black." Drinking the hot brew seemed to calm her, at least for the moment. She set down her cup. "I was about to tell you something last night when Rory came in."

A thrill of excitement shot through Maggie as she braced herself for whatever Meredith was about to say. "Yes. I'm sorry we didn't get to talk longer."

Meredith stared into space, her gaze unfocused. Then she sighed. "I've got to get this off my chest. And I really don't think my old friend wants to talk to me right now."

"You mean Daisy?"

"Yes. I don't blame her a bit for not taking my calls."

June returned and quietly set down the sugar packets and a pitcher of milk, doing her best to be unobtrusive. Maggie added a splash of milk to her cup, allowing the new widow to set the pace.

"I had a fight with Benton the night he died." Meredith's pale cheeks flushed. "Down on the docks."

"That's where we—" Maggie cut off her words. "That's where Benton was found," she quickly said.

Meredith gave her a strange look. "I know. I was there, remember?"

"That's right." Maggie shuddered. "I'm trying to forget that night, quite honestly. I seem to be succeeding somewhat." She could have kicked herself. She was trying to encourage Meredith to spill it, not deter her.

Meredith set down her mug. "I'm sorry, I didn't mean to make things worse for you."

June stepped forward. "Meredith, please. You're among friends. Feel free to confide in us."

"If it helps, I had a lot of regrets when my husband died," Maggie added. "It helped to talk about it with someone." That wasn't entirely true, but she felt a white lie was all right under the circumstances. At least she hoped so.

Meredith picked up her cup again, and Maggie relaxed at the signal that she was going to keep talking. "After dinner, I followed Benton down to the docks. I was hoping to clear the air." She paused. When she started talking again, her voice was a whisper. "He found out about Rory's interest in me." She cleared her throat. "You have to understand, things between Benton and me were complicated."

June's brows raised, and Maggie could practically read her mind. "It's complicated" was shorthand that covered a whole bunch of messy relationship issues.

"We were headed for divorce, and then we weren't, but then we were again. Both of us were ambivalent. I was hoping we could work it out."

Before or after the discovery of gold was added to the mix? Maggie wondered.

"It happens," June said in a soothing voice. "You had a long history. The important thing right now is to bring Benton's killer to justice."

"That's right," Maggie jumped in. "Did you see Benton before or after Harry Carter fought with him?"

Meredith cocked her head. "After. I passed Harry on the way to the docks. He was holding a hand over his eye." She demonstrated.

Maggie's pulse leaped. Maybe they could clear Harry. But why hadn't Meredith told the police about their encounter? "Was he wearing his coat?" At Meredith's puzzled look, she added, "A navy blue peacoat?"

"I don't think so. Our encounter was brief. We didn't even greet each other."

So Harry theoretically could have gone to the hotel, put on his coat, and returned to kill Benton. Not likely, but that was how the police might view it.

"How was Benton?" June's question was blunt.

Meredith's hands began to shake as she set her cup down again. "He was fine, more or less. He was having a real hissy fit over what he thought was going on. Nothing I said made any difference, probably because he was three sheets to the wind." She wiped tears away. "He told me to get out of his sight. I never got to tell him how much I loved him." As sobs erupted, she turned and scurried out.

Maggie and June were silent for a moment, both staring at the front door.

"What was all that?" June finally asked.

"I'm not sure," Maggie said. "Actually, I'm more confused than ever."

June leaned on the counter, one hand propping up her chin. "I can't tell if she's lying or not. Did she even go down to the docks?"

"I think she did." Maggie picked up the earrings and put them back in the case. "Right before she came in, I was going to tell you that the police found one of her earrings down there. Right where they think Benton was killed."

"Maybe she's trying to spin a story in advance of being questioned."

"Could be. She could have been fishing to see if we knew anything too."

"Either way, that was quite a performance. Whenever there are millions at stake, I'm afraid I become a little more skeptical about declarations of undying love."

"Me too." Then guilt twisted in Maggie's belly. What if Meredith had been sincere? "I hate the way murder makes me question everyone and everything."

"I hope that doesn't include me." James stepped out of the back room, wiping his hands on a rag.

"James. I didn't even know you were here." Maggie's cheeks heated. *What if I'd said something . . . personal about him?*

June winked at Maggie, clearly reading her mind. "Don't worry, I wouldn't have let that happen."

"Let what happen?" James looked puzzled. When the two women burst into laughter, he shook his head. "Never mind. It's clearly a female thing. I wanted you to know I finished gluing the veneer on that sideboard. Let it dry for a day and it will be good to go."

"Thanks, James," June said. She held up a finger as the shop phone rang. "Excuse me for a minute." She picked up the receiver and greeted the caller. "It's Ruth," she said, holding the phone out to Maggie. "She wants to talk to you."

"Maggie." Ruth's tone was brisk and businesslike. "I took the liberty of contacting a friend who works at a college library in Boston, and I've found something very enlightening. Something that could make all the difference to our investigation."

Maggie's heart gave a leap. "What is it?"

Ruth chuckled. "If it's all right with you, I'd like to call a special meeting and share it then."

"Let's have potluck at my house tonight." Maggie's mind whirred, thinking about a possible menu. "I've got a big lasagna in the freezer."

"That sounds good," Ruth said. "I'll make my garlic bread. Since you're at the shop right now, I'll take care of calling the others."

"Thanks. Come over at six." Hanging up, Maggie turned to June and James. "I hope you two can make it tonight. We're having potluck and a big reveal from Ruth."

"I can't wait," James said. "I'll bring my mother and something to share."

Fortunately the rest of the afternoon passed quickly as Maggie and June assisted customers and planned future inventory purchases. Underneath it all, anticipation thrummed, lending wings to Maggie's feet when she walked home after closing. Things were coming to a head, both with Thomas Sedgwick's story and the murder investigation. She sensed it.

As if echoing her mood, the sky was active too, with storm clouds rolling in and becoming denser by the minute. A moisture-laden wind was howling. The northeaster was about to blow.

At home, Maggie turned on the oven and pulled the pan of lasagna out of the freezer. Then she fed a whining Snickers and laid a fire in the dining room. Lit candles along the mantel and on the table provided a welcoming ambiance. She put out place mats and matching napkins and set the table with silverware. Soft classical music on the stereo was the last touch.

The doorbell rang, and soon the kitchen was filled with laughing, chattering friends. Everyone showed up except Daisy, who was at home with Harry. In addition to Ruth's bread, they had June's salad, Deborah's cookies, Ina's deviled eggs, Fran's brownies, and Liz's corn chowder. James provided wine for those who wanted it.

Once plates were loaded and carried to the dining room, Liz said grace. When everyone picked up forks and spoons, ready to dig in, Maggie put up her hand. "You all can go ahead and enjoy this wonderful food, but I'm not going to eat a single bite until Ruth shares her news."

"All right, Maggie. I don't blame you. I was too excited to eat after I got this." Ruth opened the folder she had placed on the table close at hand. She adjusted her glasses and picked up a piece of paper. "My friend was able to locate the list of men who were on the *Abigail* when it went down, including the Confederates." She paused and peered at them over her glasses to make sure she had everyone's attention before she dropped the bomb.

"One of the criminals on board was named Alfred Addison Stringfellow."

20

Maggie wasn't sure she had heard right. "Did you say Alfred Addison *Stringfellow*?"

Ina bounced up and down in her chair. "She sure did. And I bet our Addison Stringfellow is related."

"Hold on, there's more." Ruth picked up another piece of paper. "We took our research a step further and checked out the family tree. It took a lot of digging, but we learned that Professor Addison Stringfellow is a direct descendant of the Confederate who robbed the Boston bank. Addison the elder left a wife and children in Savannah, Georgia, where our Addison lives and works. In addition, according to records, Stringfellow was one of the Confederate ringleaders."

"There you have it," Liz said, stabbing her fork into the leafy green salad. "A direct connection between the *Abigail* and someone on the salvage crew."

"But does it mean anything?" Fran's cheeks pinked as everyone turned to look at her. "Maybe that's why they asked him to join the show."

"Maybe," James said. "But he's never mentioned the connection, has he, Maggie?" He selected another slice of garlic bread from the basket.

"That's true." Maggie thought back over her meetings with Addison. "He's certainly had plenty of opportunity since he was always rubbing my nose in Thomas Sedgwick's supposed involvement. And Abigail's." She wondered if Stringfellow's ancestor had been among the spies who had dined at Sedgwick Manor all those years ago. If so, surely Addison would have said so.

Unless he didn't want it known.

June picked up her phone. "Excuse me, folks, but I'm going to check something." She tapped at her phone's screen for a couple of minutes, then gave a grunt of satisfaction. "It doesn't appear that the professor ever talks about his ancestor. I've scrolled through the list of papers and presentations he's given, and—conveniently—none of them even mentions the Confederate bank robbery."

A hush fell over the table as everyone digested the news. The fire flickered as a gust came down the chimney and rain began to beat against the windowpanes. The storm had arrived.

"I'm starting to think something really far-fetched," Maggie said. "I'm wondering if Addison killed Benton. We didn't even consider him a suspect, but it seems to me he has a huge motive."

"You mean because his ancestor died in the shipwreck?" Liz asked. "He didn't want them to disturb his grave? That is far-fetched."

"Nothing so noble," Maggie said. "I think Addison wants the gold for himself. He might think he deserves it, since it was his ancestor who stole it."

Everyone began to talk at once, bouncing Maggie's theory around, either debunking or embellishing it. Ina was especially animated in her denunciation of the professor, claiming he had shifty eyes and clammy hands, two sure signs of a criminal personality. In response, Liz made the point that in that case, many of the anxious people seeking Pastor David's counsel could be labeled criminals.

James, seated to Maggie's left, whispered to her, "What do you think we should do?"

Maggie thought for a moment. "We really don't have enough evidence to go to the police. I mean, a family relationship isn't proof of guilt. Otherwise they could arrest me too." They chuckled quietly before she went on. "But I do think we need to tell Rory about this. He can take it from there." Even though Rory had fired her so abruptly, she still wanted to warn him about Addison's possible conflict of interest. That was the decent thing to do.

"I think we should talk to Robert Linton too," James said. "He can do whatever he wants with the information." He cocked his head, listening to the wind and rain. "Not much will be happening tonight. So let's enjoy our dinner first."

Maggie dug into her pasta, suddenly starving. "Good idea."

After dinner, James drove Maggie to the hotel to talk to Rory. She'd tried to call him without success, and he hadn't returned her voice mails.

"I hope he's here," Maggie said as they pulled up to the shelter of the front portico.

"Where else would he be at nine o'clock on a weekday night in Somerset Harbor?" James's voice was wry.

The valet hurried to open her door. "It's a wild night," she said to the young man, thanking him for his courtesy.

"That it is, ma'am." He caught the keys James threw to him. "Have a good night."

James followed Maggie into the warm and dry lobby. The place was quiet, with only a couple of patrons sitting by the fireplace.

"Let's check the restaurant and lounge first," James said.

"Good idea." Maggie allowed James to take the lead, thankful he was there. She had to admit to feeling some trepidation about facing Rory after their last conversation. Hopefully he wouldn't be hostile.

There was no sign of Rory in the dining room or the lounge. No one from the crew was among those dining or listening to the acoustic duo in the lounge either. Maggie understood why:

The few seconds they caught of the act was enough for her. Sea shanties weren't her thing, although they reminded her of Clem. Where was he? And *what* was he—criminal, accomplice, or victim?

"Can I help you?" The desk clerk looked up eagerly as they approached. No doubt it was a boring job on a quiet night.

"Is Rory James in?" Maggie asked with more assurance than she felt.

The young woman picked up the phone. "Who shall I say is asking?"

James stepped forward. "James Bennett, Somerset Harbor alderman."

The clerk's brows rose. "Right away, sir."

Maggie threw James a grateful look. Rory wouldn't dare ignore a summons from a town official.

The clerk frowned, shaking her head. "He's not answering. Do you want to leave a message?"

"Do we, Maggie?" James asked.

Maggie thought for a moment. She shook her head. "Follow me. Let's go see Meredith."

They thanked the helpful clerk as they started across the lobby to the elevators. "I figure we should go see her rather than call," Maggie said. "I have no idea how she will respond to seeing me."

They had to knock on the door of Room 301 several times before they heard the rattle of the door opening. Apparently in for the night, Meredith was wearing a white terry robe. "Maggie." Her puzzled gaze went to James. "And Mr. Bennett?"

"Sorry to bother you so late." Maggie glanced around the quiet hallway. "Can we come in for a minute? I promise you it's urgent."

"Of course." Fear flashed across Meredith's face as she stood back to let them enter. "Someone else hasn't, I mean . . ."

"No one else is hurt," Maggie said quickly. *That we know of,* *anyway.* "We're looking for Rory."

Meredith perched on the arm of the sofa. "What do you want with him? He won't change his mind about you being on the show, you know." Refusing to meet Maggie's gaze, she picked at a loose thread on the robe.

"I don't want him to. I want to warn him."

"That's right," James said. "We've learned that Addison Stringfellow is related to one of the Confederate bank robbers."

"And that's important why?" Meredith's eyes narrowed.

"Meredith, think about it," Maggie said. "Did you kill Benton?"

The other woman jumped up. "No, of course not. I told the police that when they brought over my earring." Her lips twisted. "They wouldn't give it to me, of course, in case they do trump up a case against me."

"Well then, did Rory kill him?" Maggie asked.

Meredith put her hands on her hips. "Oh, are you starting that again? He's ambitious, but not that ambitious."

Maggie sighed. "I wasn't accusing him. I was making the point that Addison could very well be guilty, and we wanted Rory to know about his connection to the Confederates. Since the professor has tried to hide it, or at least doesn't seem keen to share." She glanced around. "So is Rory here? The clerk said he didn't answer his phone."

"I'm sorry, he isn't. He went out aboard the *Deep Six* with Addison. Captain Gene said it was ready, so they weighed anchor a couple of hours ago."

"In this storm?" James frowned. He gestured at the tall windows, where rain was lashing the glass. "And it's dark."

Meredith shrugged. "It's always dark under the ocean. And that's where the gold is."

On the way down to the lobby in the elevator, Maggie clutched James's arm. "What should we do? I have a really bad feeling about this."

He set his lips in a grim line. "Me too. Why on earth are they on the water in this storm? Whatever gold might be down there has been there over a hundred years, and I doubt it's going anywhere."

The doors opened at the lower level to reveal Kristen, the sound tech, waiting to get on. She clutched several chocolate bars in her hands.

"Caught me," she said with a rueful grin, nodding at the chocolate.

"Kristen," Maggie said. "You're not out on the *Deep Six*?"

The young woman shook her head as she pushed past to enter the elevator. "Nope. No filming tonight. Chris and I are both grounded. Hence the chocolate. I always eat it when I'm lonely." She winked as the door began to close. "And Eric's on the boat."

"Wait a minute." Maggie stuck her foot in the door, making it open again. "Who told you not to go? Was it Rory?"

Kristen shook her head. "No. It was that professor dude." The doors closed, and the elevator began to rise.

"Now I know something is wrong," Maggie said as they crossed the lobby. "Chris said his job was to film everything. Should we call the Coast Guard?"

"That might be premature. Maybe we can get out to the boat somehow before we call in the troops." James peered out a French door. "It looks like the storm is in a lull."

Maggie snapped her fingers. "Let's call Harry."

"On it." James reached inside his jacket pocket and pulled out his phone. As the phone rang on the other end, James and Maggie moved to a secluded corner of the lobby.

"Harry," James said. "I'm with Maggie and I'm going to put you on speakerphone."

"And I've got Daisy on the extension," Harry said with a chuckle. "What's up?"

James filled Harry and Daisy in, with Maggie interjecting. "It looks like the storm has quieted. Would you be able to take us out in the lobster boat?"

Harry hissed between his teeth. "Normally I would. But I'd be breaking the terms of my bail."

"Darn. I forgot about that," James said.

"I have an idea, if you're game. You take the boat, James. Didn't you do some lobstering in high school?"

"Man, you have a good memory, Harry. One of my uncles was a lobsterman, and I used to help him. Sometimes he let me pilot the boat."

"Then it's settled. Meet you at the dock in ten."

"Really, James? You're going to take Harry's boat out?" Maggie was both excited and nervous. "I didn't know you were a lobsterman."

He held his arm out for her to take. "I'm a man of many talents, most of them hidden."

Harry was waiting at the docks by the time they arrived amid a lull in the weather. He handed James the keys. "Put on the life jackets and slickers." Tipping his head back, he studied the sky. "You got about an hour window, max, before she's going to blow again."

James jingled the keys. "We'd better hustle then."

"One more thing. You run into any trouble—any at all—you call me on the radio. I have a base station at the house. Your cells might not work out there." Harry gave them the call signs. "Good luck and Godspeed."

James helped Maggie climb aboard, and they put on their

gear. Then Maggie helped James cast off while he started the engine. The first lurch of the boat reminded Maggie of their last trip out to the shoals, when the squall had suddenly blown in. Fear clenched her belly at the idea of being out on stormy seas again.

But then she thought about Rory and the others possibly being at the mercy of a killer. Who else was going to investigate?

Maggie took a deep breath of briny air. This was an adventure, right?

James edged the *Daisy Mae* out of her berth and eased her out into the harbor. Spotlights illuminated their way out of the inner waters, enabling them to avoid other boats where they rocked on their moorings.

Once they reached open water and James increased their speed, he turned to her. "I'd forgotten how much fun this is—under better circumstances, of course."

A display with a moving chart showed their progress across the bay. Their destination, the shoals, was indicated as a hazard to avoid.

Overhead the cloud cover was thick, blocking any sight of moon or stars. Maggie shivered. The air was cold even though they were protected under the canopy from most of the wind. How much longer until the storm returned in force?

The *Daisy Mae* thrust steadily through the water, the lighthouse's beam their only companion. Maggie had never been on the water at night, and the emptiness of sea and sky was like a physical sensation. She thought of Thomas Sedgwick and his many voyages. In those days there hadn't been phones or radios. How had he endured the loneliness? And when a ship did go down, there were usually no witnesses. The boat would literally disappear without a trace.

Maggie shook herself. They weren't alone out here. Harry

knew where they were. As if in answer to her thoughts, the radio crackled. *"Daisy Mae,* come in, *Daisy Mae.* What's your position?" Harry's voice was like the first sight of home.

James picked up the microphone and gave the coordinates as well as an overview of the conditions. Despite years away from the water after a bad boating accident that had taken the life of his high school sweetheart, he obviously remembered the protocols.

"Making good time," Harry said. "Call me when you reach your destination."

"Will do," James said. "Over and out."

Maggie spotted the *Deep Six* on the horizon. The ship was well lit by the running lights and beacons on the antennas. "There she is," she called, shouting to be heard over the engine.

James nodded and adjusted the boat's trajectory slightly. "It's going to get choppier out here because of the shoals," he called, "and I'm going to slow down so they don't hear us. We might wallow a bit." The engine slowed to a grumbling hum.

Maggie watched in admiration as James deftly handled the boat, bringing the *Daisy Mae* around so the two boats lined up perfectly at the stern. As they tied off to one of the hitching rings, cold rain began to lash down again, stinging Maggie's face.

"We're in for it now," James said. He grabbed the radio and called Harry, giving him an update on their coordinates and the weather conditions. "If we don't call you again in fifteen minutes, call the Coast Guard."

Maggie stared up at the ladder, daunted once again by the steep and narrow rungs. Worse, this time they were slick with rain.

James moved to her side. "I'll go up behind you. Don't worry, Maggie, I won't let you fall." He gave her a hug and a pat on the back, urging her forward.

Closing her eyes briefly, she shot up a prayer. Then she attacked the ladder, determined to get the ordeal over with before fear had a chance to paralyze her limbs. It wasn't easy, dressed as she was in the bulky life jacket and slicker, but after a few tense, focused minutes, the deck was within reach.

James slipped over the railing behind her. He grabbed her arm and tugged her down to crouch behind a piece of equipment. "Crew member," he whispered. Hunkered in the shadows, Maggie held her breath as one of the sailors strolled along the deck toward them, whistling.

As he passed under a spotlight, James gasped. "He's armed."

Maggie squinted her eyes. Light glinted off something slung over the man's shoulder. *A rifle.* "What are we going to do?" she whispered.

"Hold on, I have an idea." James cat-footed around a container, vanishing from Maggie's view. The man continued to approach, seeming to beeline for the rear of the boat. If he reached the railing, he would spot the *Daisy Mae* tied up below. And if he peered into the shadows, he would see her. Her skin prickled with vulnerability.

"Oof!" The man flew forward, hitting his forehead hard on the deck as he fell. James had tackled him. The alderman wrestled the limp sailor to a seated position against the railing, where he slumped, unconscious. To Maggie's amazement, James pulled a strap out of his slicker and bound the man's hands.

"That will slow him down, but he may not be out long." James grimaced. "I didn't mean to hit him so hard. I guess adrenaline kicked in." He slipped the rifle off the man's shoulder and hid it behind a stack of metal containers. "I don't want this falling into the wrong hands."

"Good thinking," Maggie whispered. "Where did you get the strap you used to tie him up?"

"From Harry's boat." James stood, fists clenched, looking around. "Where do you think everyone is?"

"If they're bringing up gold, then they're below in the operations center." Maggie padded around the deck, checking the equipment. "Spot is missing. See the cable?" The boom arm was over the water and the cable was hanging down, an indication the remotely operated vehicle was in use. "Spot is the ROV they use to search and retrieve artifacts from the ocean floor."

"Then there isn't much time." James pulled out his phone. "No bars. It was a long shot that cells would work out here anyway. We'll have to call Harry on the radio and tell him to get the Coast Guard over here. There's no reason that crewman should have been patrolling with a gun." He raised his hood against the rain, which had begun to pour down in earnest. "They're not going to be happy coming out in this."

Maggie regarded the *Daisy Mae*, rolling on her mooring, with trepidation. "I'm not happy one of us needs to climb down there in this downpour."

James hesitated. "Maggie, I know you hate that ladder, but I really think I should be the one to guard this guy. I don't want to leave you alone up here."

"You're right." Maggie moved toward the railing. "I'll be okay. Say a little prayer for me."

She climbed down easily enough, timing her jump into the boat just right as it bobbed in the swells. "*Daisy Mae* to base," she said into the radio. Hopefully the howling wind would prevent her voice from carrying to the deck of the *Deep Six*. Unfortunately that also meant she couldn't hear if James was in trouble.

Harry answered right away. "Come in, *Daisy Mae*. I was getting ready to call in the troops."

"I think you'd better. We've got a situation out here. The crew members are armed."

The radio gave a squawk. "Armed, you say? Hang on, the Coast Guard will be there shortly."

"And base? The weather is deteriorating."

"I know, I've been watching the maps. Be careful. Over and out."

Maggie put the handset back in its slot. An especially large wave hit the lobster boat, sending her flying. She grabbed the edge of the canopy and held on until it settled.

She'd have to time her ascent between waves. Staring upward with the driving rain soaking her face, Maggie waited. At the right moment, she grabbed a rung and began to climb. As before, she focused on moving her hands and feet without thinking too much about what she was actually doing or the surging ocean below.

One step up. Two. Three—

One foot slipped off the rung. Then the other. Maggie was hanging by her bare hands. The ocean surged below, sending spray up to drench her legs.

Panic made her heart race, and her hands grew even more slippery with fear. *Lord, help!* With a huge effort that made her legs shake, she hauled her left sneaker back up onto the rung, then the right one.

She rested for a minute, gasping for air, willing the oxygen to calm her pulse and clear her head. Then she forced herself to climb, step by careful step, making sure her grip and her footing were secure before moving.

Finally she achieved the top, relief rushing through her limbs. She swung her leg over the railing—and came face to face with the barrel of a gun.

Maggie gasped, managing only by sheer force of will to hang on to the railing. As her vision cleared, she saw it was one of the sailors training his weapon on her. *Where is James?*

The stranger grabbed her arm and tugged her the rest of the way onto the boat. "Come on. We've got your boyfriend waiting for you." He sneered at her. With a shove he sent her stumbling across the deck. She slipped and almost fell on the wet surface.

"Maggie." Captain Gene stood in the open doorway to the bridge. "Good to see you again." His tone was jocular as always, but he was frowning.

"Where's James?" Maggie heard her voice shaking. The crewmen moved closer, herding her toward the doorway. What were they going to do?

The captain made a dismissive gesture. "Don't worry about him. He's all right." He stood aside so she could see James, tied to a chair. The beginnings of a black eye marred the left side of his face.

Maggie gasped and ran toward him. "Are you all right, James?" She bent closer and pretended to kiss his cheek. Instead she whispered, "They're on their way."

He slid his gaze toward her in acknowledgement of her message. "I'm okay." His voice was raspy.

"Lucky for him my guy is okay too." Captain Gene crossed his arms. "Tie her up," he said to the man following Maggie.

Maggie submitted to having her hands tied and feet bound to a chair next to James. She did her best to remain calm, praying feverishly that the Coast Guard would hurry to their rescue. Hopefully the intensifying storm wouldn't hamper them.

Addison Stringfellow appeared in the doorway. His expression filled with wicked delight when he spotted Maggie and James. "What do we have here, Gene?"

The captain chuckled. "A couple of Yankees stickin' their noses in where they're not wanted."

"They're good at that." Addison sauntered into the room. "Too bad they won't be able to use what they've learned."

"You two are working together, aren't you?" Maggie blurted. "In fact, you made sure Captain Gene was hired on, didn't you, Addison? And I'll bet you two are responsible for all the 'troubles' the project has experienced." It all made sense now. Once Captain Gene was hired, he had been able to put his own crew in place. A shiver went down her spine. Had they caused the captain's mugging and the car accident that put an original crew member out of commission? And there had been disaster after disaster with the boat. The motor, the fire, the equipment breakdowns—anything to delay the retrieval of the gold.

The professor leaned back against a table, crossing his arms. "You're a smart one, Maggie. Too bad you didn't figure it out a little sooner." His grin was a taunting leer.

Maggie was tempted to blurt out that the Coast Guard was coming to arrest them, but a glance from James stifled the urge. They needed to keep the criminals occupied until help arrived. She sent the two men her best glare. "I'll bet one of you killed Benton too."

Captain Gene chuckled as he jerked a thumb at Addison. "That was all him. Wasn't my idea."

Addison's face reddened, and he clenched his fists. "You're the one who said Benton was figuring things out, that he was in the way."

Captain Gene grunted in derision. "I didn't tell you to kill the man, you fool. We don't need police attention comin' down on us." He gestured at Maggie and James. "And now we have other people snooping around."

The professor's glance at Maggie and James was dismissive. "Oh, we can take care of them easily enough. Just another boating accident during a storm."

Maggie's stomach turned over. All the men had to do was scuttle the lobster boat with them aboard, tied up and unable to help themselves. In cold Maine waters, death would come quickly. That was the only mercy. Beside her, James writhed and groaned, and Maggie had the sense he was restraining himself. But she couldn't. "You won't get away with it," she said. "The police will figure out you killed Benton."

"Right." Addison's expression was smug. "I wore Harry's coat and used his whaling lance." He jabbed a thumb into his chest. "There's nothing to connect his death with me."

"You had better hope not." Captain Gene made a cutting motion across his throat. "I'm not goin' down for that one."

Addison glared at his partner, but before he could say anything, another crew member appeared in the doorway. "We're bringing Spot up. He has the gold!"

The captain and Addison began to run out of the room. Before he exited, Addison called back over his shoulder, "Don't go anywhere, you two." He grinned malevolently.

As soon as they disappeared, James turned to Maggie. "Quick, untie me." He scooted his chair toward her, turning his back. The criminals had used chairs with wheels, an oversight Maggie was sure they would regret but of which she would take full advantage.

When she reached for James's hands, she was surprised to feel something cold and slippery in her palm. A small penknife. "You're a genius. How did you hide that?"

"In my fist. See if you can open it without dropping it. I know it will be tricky."

Holding her breath and praying, Maggie tugged at the blade with her fingertips. Fortunately the knife was easy to open. "Okay, I'm ready."

"I'm pulling my hands apart as far as I can," James said. "I was able to build in some slack when they tied me. Cut in the middle."

Maggie did as he said, clutching the knife in her fist and sawing at the rope. At the same time, James pulled his hands apart to make the line taut and easier to cut. "I think I've got it!" She felt the knife cut through the last strands. "Should I do another piece?"

James wiggled his hands. "No, that was enough." He turned around in the chair and took the knife from Maggie's fingers. "I'll do your hands after I free my feet." A few grunts, then Maggie felt his hands on hers. "Pull your hands apart as far as possible. And hold still."

Maggie complied, feeling the rope bite into her wrists. The tugging of the knife as it sliced the thick strands made it hurt even more, but she bit back a cry of pain. Finally she felt blessed freedom as the rope parted and released her wrists. James spun her around and cut her feet free.

"Thank you." She wiggled her feet and rubbed her wrists to restore blood flow. "Now what?"

"We're out of here." James rose to his feet with a groan.

Maggie glanced out of the large window, where shouting figures clustered around the ROV device as it was lowered to the deck. "But we can't get to the lobster boat."

James tugged at her arm. "We aren't using the lobster boat." He led her through a different door out of the bridge and onto the forward deck. Here dinghies dangled from their hoists.

"What's the plan, James? Aren't we going to help Rory and the technicians?"

After inspecting the dinghy, James found a switch and flipped it. The boat began to swing out over the side. "We don't know who is involved. Rory could be one of the gang stealing the gold. If not, then someone is probably guarding him. We can't risk it."

Maggie regarded the boat with dismay. It had been bad enough plowing through stormy seas in the *Daisy Mae*. This frail craft looked like it might easily be swamped. "You don't think we should wait for the Coast Guard?"

"No way. We don't know how fast they'll get here." He grimaced at her. "My job is to get you home safe. I shouldn't have brought you in the first place."

"It's as much my fault as yours. I wanted to come."

James craned his neck toward the far deck. "No time to argue. Hop in."

Maggie obeyed, scrambling over the side and into the boat. James followed.

"Now what?" she asked.

"This." James found the control box on a spring-loaded wire, continuing to lower the boat toward the water. Maggie peered over the side. Light from the lower decks shone on the black water, which was pitching and tossing. Another gust of wind and rain shook the dinghy, making it sway. Reaching under her slicker, she tightened the straps of her life jacket, grateful she was wearing one.

The boat nestled into the waves with a lurch that forced Maggie to clutch the side. James released the lines, and the boom arm moved back up toward the deck.

They were adrift in the turbulent water, the waves and current hurling them toward the rocks that had wrecked the *Abigail*.

22

"Hang on!" James shouted as he started the engine. The engine caught immediately, to Maggie's gratitude. But despite the motor's horsepower, they continued to be pulled toward Deadmen's Shoals, which brought them alongside the stern of the ship.

Someone shouted, and a spotlight swung over the water, catching them in the beam. Maggie squinted against the light, feeling like a sitting duck. "Can they shoot us from that distance?"

"I sure hope not." He turned the lever, forcing the engine to strain against the current as he attempted to take them out of range.

Maggie heard shouts on deck and saw men scuffling in the dim yellow light that illuminated the scene. Then one figure was pushed over the railing. She screamed, "James, man overboard!"

The man flailed in the waves, his face a lighter oval against the dark water. The spotlight swung to him and Maggie saw it was Addison, his glasses missing and gasping for air, one hand raised above the surface. Worse, no one from the ship was attempting to help him.

"James, we need to save him." Even if Addison was a killer and a kidnapper, Maggie couldn't sit back and watch him drown.

"Throw him that life preserver." James pointed to a striped circular flotation device attached to a rope.

After making sure the life preserver was attached to the boat securely, Maggie wound up and threw it toward the drowning man, sending it as far as she could with a prayer.

By a miracle, it landed right beside him. Addison grabbed it and Maggie began to tug the rope, pulling him toward them. With any luck, he would survive to face justice.

James gave a shout, pointing. Maggie turned to see a well-lit Coast Guard cutter bearing down on them, arriving like an angel of mercy out of the dark, stormy night.

. . . .

"Here it is—the moment of truth," June said as Maggie prepared to open the metal tube. During the x-ray of the figurehead, an object had been spotted after being hidden for over a century.

"Are you ready, everyone?" Maggie asked, glancing at the others circling the table. In addition to June, James and the other members of the historical society were in the audience. Rory and Stella were sharing cohost duties since the event was to be filmed by both television programs. Today Maggie had two cameras to worry about, making sure she ignored them as directed.

"Ready when you are, mate," Rory said. The ordeal on the ship had only temporarily dampened his cockiness. Now he was fielding offers from networks for a brand-new adventure show and had accepted one such offer that morning.

"Roll 'em," Meredith said from her position on the side. With the departure of Rory, she was going to take over Benton's show. The technicians and film crew were staying.

Daisy gave her old friend a thumbs-up sign. Earlier in the day as she did Maggie's makeup for the shoot, she had told Maggie about the air-clearing lunch she'd had with Meredith. "I can't believe she thought I was purposely not taking her calls," she'd said. "Meredith had the wrong phone number for me, but we got that fixed right up. She always was a bit silly in that way."

Maggie took a deep breath. Whatever was inside the tube could mean everything—or nothing.

The tube easily came apart in her hand, having been treated along the seam with chemicals to loosen the corrosion. Everyone gasped when rolled papers wrapped in oilcloth slid out onto the blotter.

"What do you think these papers are?" Stella asked.

As prearranged, Maggie said, "I hope they're the missing pages from Captain Sedgwick's logbook. The last entries—for the days of the robbery and the shipwreck—are missing." The cameras zoomed in on the logbook, laid flat to display the defaced area.

With shaking fingers, Maggie picked up the log pages and unrolled them. With June's help, she flattened them out and set paperweights on the corners to hold them in place. The first few pages recounted the days before the robbery, when the *Abigail* was docked in Boston Harbor.

"'September 12, 1864,'" Maggie read. A chill went down her spine, and she sensed the tension in the audience. She skipped over the weather data to the remarks section.

> *Meeting with Mr. Edwards at the bank regarding my note. While there, a band of ruffians entered, demanding gold. To my dismay, they seemed to have followed me, since they called out to me and insisted on accompanying me back to the Abigail. One man, named Stringfellow, was especially impertinent and rude.*

"So it ran in the family," Ina observed, to the amusement of all.

Professor Addison Stringfellow and Captain Gene were in jail, along with Gene's crew. Their present-day robbery had been foiled with the arrival of the Coast Guard. Although Addison was all right after his cold-water dip, the shock of being thrown overboard by his partner had led him to confess everything in hopes of implicating the captain. In turn the captain had claimed to be merely a hired hand and insisted that Addison going into the water had been an accident. Addison was also the thief who had stolen the lap desk and Abigail's papers, both of which had been retrieved from his room at the Oceanside to Maggie's great relief. Captain Gene had been responsible for locking Maggie in Clem's shed.

The only winners in the episode were Benton's investors—who'd received a handsome fee for the treasure—and the network. A reenactment of the retrieval of the gold would be released as a special episode called *Deep Sea Secrets: Pirates Edition*. Media coverage and audience anticipation were already intense.

Maggie continued:

> *Stringfellow appears to be the ringleader of this motley and insalubrious crew . . .*

Everyone chuckled as she resumed:

> *. . . and despite my warnings, has ordered me to weigh anchor and sail for Canada. The weather is deteriorating fast and we'll have squalls by morning. But I am a prisoner aboard my own ship and can do nothing.*

She paused, thinking about how horrible it must have been for Thomas, compelled to sail into a terrible storm. It must have gone against every instinct as a captain, especially when criminals were giving the orders.

Rory stepped in with a remark about the weather-predicting capabilities captains needed to have in those days. "Of course, once they were in it, they didn't have much recourse. There wasn't any communication with the mainland."

Maggie went on:

Worse, he is forcing us to betray our president and our country. But it is either comply with hope of salvation later, or die now at their hands. I must think of my crew and not my pride.

"What a terrible dilemma." Rory shook his head.

"Thomas Sedgwick was not in league with the thieves," Stella said. "He was hijacked."

The entry for the next morning was dire.

We've taken on water and are sinking fast. As feared, the wind, waves, and current pushed us toward the shoals, which tear at our craft like jagged teeth. I've sent men in the lifeboats with prayers that they will survive.

Maggie paused, her throat tightening.

May God go with them. And may He look kindly upon my soul and forgive my sins. And if ever my wife Abigail reads these words, may she know that she was well loved and always in my thoughts, especially now, as I stand at the gateway to eternal life. Yours truly, Thomas Sedgwick.

Maggie fell silent, touched to the core by Thomas's words. The others around her were also quiet, seeming to feel that same reverence.

The rattle of the shop door disturbed their silence. Robert Linton entered, stopping short when he saw the gathering and the cameras. "I'm sorry, I didn't mean to interrupt."

"Cut," Meredith called. "Time for a break anyway. That was perfect, Maggie. Good job."

The group dispersed, breaking into chatter while Maggie

approached the police officer. "How are you, Robert?"

Robert glanced behind her. "I'm sorry to interrupt," he said again, "but I've found out who left the skeleton and the box of feathers." His lips twisted in bemusement. "It was a couple of high school kids. They thought it was real funny to play pranks on you after they heard the rumors about Captain Sedgwick."

"They were harmless." In light of the other threats she'd faced, those incidents seemed almost funny.

"Maybe so, but they still have to do a service project. Is there anything you need done around here?"

"Not here. But I do have an idea for a project." Fortunately, Clem Jenkins had been found unharmed—but plenty angry—in one of the *Deep Six* cabins. He'd been kidnapped by Addison when he'd caught the professor trying to plant the murder weapon at the old man's shanty. "I think Clem's house could use some work. Let's get a group together." Maybe an outpouring of concern and help from the town would convince Clem that the jinx was truly lifted at last.

Maggie glanced at the portraits of Thomas and Abigail, brought over from the house for the filming. She smiled. The shadow over their love and devotion had also been lifted.

To discover all that country decorating has to offer and see the creative home decorating tips that inspire Maggie and her friends, check out the latest issue of *Country Sampler* at CountrySampler.com!